W9-BNC-611

Under the Egg

Under the Egg

Laura Marx Fitzgerald

Dial Books for Young Readers
An imprint of Penguin Group (USA) LLC

DIAL BOOKS FOR YOUNG READERS
Published by the Penguin Group
Penguin Group (USA) LLC, 375 Hudson Street, New York, New York 10014

USA/Canada/UK/Ireland/Australia/New Zealand/India/South Africa/China
PENGUIN.COM
A Penguin Random House Company

Library of Congress Cataloging-in-Publication Data
Fitzgerald, Laura Marx.
  Under the egg / by Laura Marx Fitzgerald.
    pages cm
  Summary: Her grandfather's dying words lead thirteen-year-old Theodora Tenpenny
to a valuable, hidden painting she fears may be stolen, but it is her search for answers in
her Greenwich Village neighborhood that brings a real treasure.
  ISBN 978-0-8037-4001-3 (hardcover)
  [1. Neighborhoods—Fiction. 2. Art—Fiction. 3. Friendship—Fiction. 4. Recluses—
Fiction. 5. Holocaust, Jewish (1939–1945)—Fiction. 6. Greenwich Village (New York
N.Y.)—Fiction. 7. Mystery and detective stories.] I. Title.
  PZ7.F575357Und 2014   [Fic]—dc23
2013017790

Printed in the United States of America

10 9 8 7 6 5

Designed by Jennifer Kelly
Text set in ITC New Baskerville Std

For Eleanor

Chapter One

It was the find of the century.

Or so I thought at the time.

This was back when a great day meant finding a toaster oven on the curb with a sign reading WORKS GOOD. Or scoring a bag of day-old danishes (slightly stale), which taste like heaven after months of plain oatmeal.

Manhattan's treasures aren't hard to find. You just have to look. Ignore the skyscrapers and shop windows for a minute, and look down. You'll see, people here shed possessions like dandruff. I'm not complaining. I've found clothes, toys, school supplies, enough books to open my own library branch. The sidewalks of New York are like an outdoor shopping mall where everything is free.

One time I found two Barneys bags full of moth-eaten cashmere sweaters. It only took $3.25 in quarters to shrink them at the Laundromat, and I was able to use the thick, felted wool to make a new winter jacket, stuffed with feathers from some old down pillows. All the leftover sweater arms I sewed together into leggings. The scraps I patched into a schoolbag with my name, Theodora Tenpenny, embroidered with thread I pulled out of a hotel sewing kit I found in my grandfather's dresser.

Another time I found a mint-condition snowboard. It makes a decent bookshelf.

Of course, this was back when I thought the greatest things you could find on the streets of New York were things.

But I'm getting ahead of myself.

I was coming back from the hardware store on one of those sweltering July days when you can't decide which is hotter: the sun beating down on you or the pavement radiating beneath you. From the sticky sound of each step, I could tell that the soles of my sneakers were starting to melt. What was left of my sneakers, that is.

My Keds had seen me through the seventh grade, but they couldn't keep up with my summer growth spurt. I'd already slit the canvas to free my toes and strained the laces to their limit, but as I flapped my way past Hudson Street's Korean tapas bars and be-spoke bicycle boutiques, it was clear that something had to give. Most likely the seams.

By then I saw it. Just as I turned the corner onto our street, Spinney Lane.

A pair of shoes, perched on top of a mailbox. Not the neighborhood's usual discarded pair of glamour queen high heels, but sneakers, brand-new and, on closer inspection, exactly my size: 5½ extra wide. Yes, the colors were garish, and the owner had, for some reason, hand-painted them with graffiti. But they fit. That's all that mattered.

I grabbed them before they could attract any competition, and peeling my skirt (really a yellowed cotton petticoat I'd found in the attic) off my sweaty thighs, I plopped down on the hot curb. But as I pulled off my Keds, I could hear my grandfather Jack's voice: "What? Plenty of life in those shoes! Well, if you must, here—hand me those laces. I can find a use for them."

I stopped for a moment to savor my treasure-finding triumph, when the taxi in front of me peeled away, revealing a dark, sticky spot in the middle of the street.

At first glance, you'd think it was an oil spill or gum burned black by the sun.

It had only been a couple of months ago, but it felt like years already. I had rounded Spinney Lane, as I always did on my way home from school. But this time, I saw that the street was at a standstill behind a barricade of ambulances and police cars. Truck horns blared and whined. A bike messenger and cabdriver pointed fingers and cursed in various languages. I peered into the middle of the commotion and saw . . . Jack. He was lying on the ground, thick, red blood puddled underneath him.

My own blood went cold.

It didn't matter how fast I ran to him. He was already halfway gone.

As soon as my face crossed into his line of vision, he struggled to lift his head. "It's under the egg," he rasped, his once–icy blue eyes now foggy. "Look under the egg."

The EMTs told me to keep him talking. "What is, Jack?" I said, my mind whirling between the things I knew I should say and the things I really needed to ask. "What's under the egg?"

"There's . . . a letter." His speech became more labored as blood gurgled up through his lips. "And a treasure." He closed his eyes, summoning the strength to whisper, "Before it's too late."

The rest of the day exists only in fragments. The

ambulance ride. The young doctor's sweaty hand on my shoulder. The police escort home, despite my insistence that I was perfectly all right to walk. The strange little song my mom hummed as the cops spoke to her. I knew that she had stopped listening and returned to the theorems in her head.

That was the day the Tenpennys of 18 Spinney Lane went from three to two. And really from two to one. Because without Jack, everything we had now weighed on me.

Which is why Jack told me, with his last words, where to find the one thing that would change everything.

Chapter Two

Eighteen Spinney Lane is easy to find. Just cast your eyes past the row of gleaming town houses, with their uniform brick facades and polished brass plaques and, in some cases, packs of paparazzi.

Then find the one house that looks like the residents are ready to just pack it in and get that condo in Florida.

That's ours.

It wasn't always like this. Great-great-great-great-grandfather Tenpenny made a fortune in shipping and found himself an elegant street (formerly a hardscrabble thicket, or "spinney") to build himself not one, but two town houses: one for his wife and children, and an adjoining one for his mother, complete with connecting doorways on each floor.

As it turns out, this building boom represented the peak of the Tenpenny fortune, and a year later the adjoining town house had been rented out and Grandma moved in with the rest of the family. As time went on, Greenwich Village was abandoned as the city's elite moved farther and farther uptown, but we Tenpennys stayed put.

On that hot July day, I used my new sneakers to kick the business cards and flyers ("Dear Occupant, Do you need cash—and quick? Let Town Home Realty handle your home sale!") off the stoop and jiggled the front door's brass doorknob until it finally surrendered.

No warm welcome here. Just the hot, stale parlor, silent and thick with the smell of musty books and last winter's pop-in from a stray cat. With Jack by my side, the room held a certain artistic-eccentric charm: an antique desk repaired with an oak branch in place of a leg, an ottoman made out of Yellow Pages bound together with sailor's knots, autumn leaves ironed between sheets of waxed paper and wallpapered around the room. But now, alone, with the autumn leaves drifting to the ground as the glue gave out, the place just looked odd, like a stylish great-aunt who has begun wearing her wig backward.

A breeze from the dining room windows brought

in the clucking of our backyard chickens, probably thirsty and impatient for dinner. Jack had started a little garden plot back there in the Great Depression, and now that garden had taken over the entire lot, including not just rows of veggies, but an apple tree, a raspberry bush, and a well-built coop for a fine flock of chickens.

At least for now. I'd lost one this week to a Jurassic-sized rat. Camille had been a tough old broad; she could've taken that rat. But since Jack died, I think we'd all had the fight knocked out of us.

The grandfather clock in the corner struck five low tones. The chickens would have to wait. It was teatime.

The stairs to the second floor creaked under my weight, made heavier by the tarnished silver tray with hard-boiled eggs and a chipped teapot, which I carried like a waitress.

Using my free hand, I gave three knocks. No answer.

Mom didn't so much as glance up from her desk as I pushed my way in. From the door I could see beads of sweat running down the back of her neck, below a knot of straw-colored hair bound up absently with a pencil. She wore her terry-cloth bathrobe, even in the stifling, dank room, with its scent of fermenting tea bags and dirty laundry.

"I've got your tea." I set the tray on the floor next to her chair. Mom got pretty agitated if I put anything on her desk, which was blanketed in yellow papers filled with numbers and cryptic characters.

She said nothing and continued scratching a pencil on her latest legal pad.

Jack said my mom was always a bit "off," even as a little girl. It's not that she was crazy or even slow. It's just that she always preferred the world inside her mind to the world outside.

I can understand this, not having much to do with the neighborhood kids myself. I've never met one who could even tell you the difference between a standard and a Phillips head. But Jack said Angelika was different than all that. She used to go out, help with chores, go to school. Her teachers and professors used words like "genius" and "extraordinarily gifted." But as the years went by, she withdrew deeper and deeper within herself, and now here she was, at her childhood desk in her childhood room, working on a dissertation that NYU stopped expecting over fifteen years ago.

Since Jack's death, she'd started refusing to leave her desk at all, save for her daily morning walk to the tea shop, where she religiously collected every variety they sold. But I caught her last week trying to leave the house in her bathrobe, so clearly things were going south.

My dad I don't know at all. My mother barely did either. Jack said he was a grifter who seduced my mom just to get his hands on the deed to our house. He sent the guy running.

I started to gather up the stray teacups from the windowsill, crouching to snag a few from under the bed.

"How's the dissertation going, Mom?"

Scritch scratch.

"Solving any theorems?"

"Well, I thought I'd made a breakthrough, but clearly the unique factorization approach won't work." She shook her head, never looking up from her notepad. "Unique factorization. Silly."

"Huh." I sat down on the bed and its tangle of sheets. "Mom, have you given any more thought to what we talked about? About selling the house? We could get a lot of money for it, I think. And we could get an apartment somewhere else in the city, maybe Brooklyn or Queens or somewhere cheaper like that."

Mom's pencil paused in the air, and she turned her sallow face slowly to stare at me. "What house?" she asked, her voice low.

"Um, this one?"

She dropped her pencil, her hands shaking. "Sell this house? But where would I work? My desk has always been right here. It's the perfect place; I can see the birds in the tree outside. See their nest? That's just where I look when I am working on an equation. And my bed is right here," she waved her hand in my direction, "in the perfect spot, so the light can fall on my pillow in the morning. Sell the house? No, no, no, it's just not possible." Her voice became higher and thinner as she shook her head wildly, and I noticed she had started winding a loose thread from her bathrobe tightly around one finger. "And where would I buy my tea? Madame Dumont always has the perfect blend ready—"

"Okay, Mom, okay. We're not going anywhere," I broke in. "Not yet."

"Because all my papers are here, my archives, you see." She frantically pawed the piles and scraps that surrounded her. "And I still have to organize them, put them in order, and my footnotes—"

"We're not selling the house, okay?" I stood up

brusquely, knocking two teacups off her book-cluttered night table, which rolled under the bed. "But, Mom, I'm serious. We can't afford all this." My hand waved over the mess, as if I were surveying the Taj Mahal. "And when winter comes, there's the gas bill and the electric bill. I'm not sure how much longer the boiler is going to hold out. How are we going to pay for that?"

Now she was humming again.

"Mom, are you sure Jack didn't mention anything about a secret stash? Somewhere he would have hidden—I don't know, money? Jewels? You know, like a treasure?"

No answer.

I began to collect the teacups again. "Should I bring up some dinner in a little while?"

I looked up to see her dangling the Lipton tea bag in front of her eyes, hot drops of tea splattering the papers that carpeted the floor. "Where's my vanilla Rooibos?"

"The Rooibos tea is gone, Mom. And that's what I'm talking about. You can't buy these expensive teas from the shop anymore. I got this kind for you—"

"But vanilla Rooibos is my afternoon tea. It's made with Madagascar vanilla, which is the finest vanilla, at least that's what Madame Dumont says. I'll get some more in the morning. Madame Dumont said she'd have a new shipment of Golden Assam ready for me . . ."

I closed the door behind me as my mother began to methodically categorize the differences between Indian and Chinese tea leaves.

After tending to the garden, the chickens, and some clogged gutters, I took my own dinner to the top floor and the room that was once Jack's studio. Jack and I had traditionally sat down together in the old dining room, where we'd spoon up our rice and beans on the Tenpenny china and then send our dishes back down to the kitchen in the dumbwaiter. But now the big dining table felt cold, even in the heat, and I preferred to eat somewhere more filled with Jack's presence.

The studio was stuffy with paint fumes, and I cracked the tall windows that lined the studio's back wall, letting in the relative cool of early evening and snatches of rush hour car horns. From my favorite spot on the long window seat, you could see the block's patchwork of yards below and catch glimpses of the Hudson River. Sometimes I'd sit and watch the pigeon flocks swoop back and forth over the rooftops. Funny how something so ragged on its own can become so beautiful when banded together.

As I ate, I riffled through the mail I'd brought up with me. One official-looking letter, with a large seal featuring an American eagle, fell to the floor. The return address: the Department of Veteran Affairs.

To whom it may concern:

The Department of Veterans Affairs was recently alerted of the death of

JOHN THORNTON TENPENNY V.

This letter is to notify you that all existing and future VA pension benefits will be hereby terminated.

Please accept our condolences at this time of your bereavement. Mr. Tenpenny's sacrifice and service to his country are deeply appreciated.

Sincerely yours,

Roger D. Fowlke
DEPARTMENT OF VETERANS AFFAIRS

I read the letter several times over. Veterans Affairs? When I did my sixth-grade history fair project on World War II, Jack told me he sat out the whole thing on account of his asthma. It seemed strange that the VA would hand out pensions to 4-Fs with breathing issues.

More to the point, the letter meant that Jack had run the household with money I'd never known about. Money that had now dried up.

I put the letter down and reached for a Mason jar, tucked in with assorted paint cans and bottles of paint thinner. The jar had once held some sky blue paint, now dried and opaque, which hid the bills and coins inside. Jack had always kept five hundred dollars in this jar, spending it down to the pennies, and then replenishing with a fresh five hundred from some unknown source.

Once, when I was around five, Jack caught me trying to sneak some change out to buy a candy bar. He roared—the only time he ever directed his famous temper at me—enraged more by the betrayal than the theft. "But it's a magic jar," I gasped between my sobs. "You take money out, and it always comes back." He got down on one knee, his strong, paint-flecked hands gripping my shoulders. "It's not magic. It's hard work that fills that jar. The hard work of earning the money, and the harder work of keeping it." His hands moved to my cheeks, wiping the tears into his calloused palms. "Now, don't cry, sister. You'll see—I'll make sure there's always money to be found."

Tonight I poured out the jar's contents and counted it again—$384. On the day Jack died, there had been $463. I guess I was lucky that he died only a week after refilling the jar. From that day forward, I had done the hard work of keeping what we had: eating only from the garden and the pantry, avoiding our few functional appliances even as the red-lined utility bills kept streaming through the mail slot. I'd even given up the Laundromat, hand-washing my sweaty clothes in the kitchen sink and drying them on the backyard line.

Still, no matter how hard I worked, the money couldn't hold out forever. Jack was right—the only magic around here was the money's disappearing act.

That left us only one lifeline: Jack's promised "treasure." I popped a last raspberry in my mouth and crossed over to the studio's defunct fireplace, where atop a grand marble mantel a chicken egg sat in a small ceramic bowl.

My first official chore in the Tenpenny house had

been the placement of that egg. Every morning, Jack and I would gather the chickens' output and select the whitest, most perfect egg of the lot. The rest of the half dozen or so went to the kitchen. The egg of honor went to the mantel. Jack would lift me in his arms, and I'd gently place the egg in the bowl made by my grandmother, a woman I knew only through Jack's stories of her skill at the potter's wheel and her fine Scandanavian cooking.

"A new day, a new beginning, a new chance at a new ending," Jack would intone solemnly. It was as close as he ever got to morning prayers.

The egg would sit in its place of honor through the day until it was replaced by the next morning's selection, when it joined the other eggs in the kitchen. But for that one day, its only job was to echo the painting above it. One of Jack's earliest pieces, the canvas was an abstract, a dark swirling abyss of midnight blues, black like charred wood, and gray like the dawn. And floating in this void was a stark white oval that haloed the real egg below.

Canvases came and went in Jack's studio—sold, lent, shown—but this one stayed above the mantel, supervising the Changing of the Egg each morning. Jack said he'd never sell it. I don't think I ever saw him so much as move it for dusting.

That was before The Spot on Spinney Street. And his last words.

Since then, every night after dinner, I worked into the last moments of the day's light to find out whether there was anything "under the egg" at all.

Maybe "under the egg" was just the last random outburst of a blood-soaked brain. But Jack always said he'd take care of me. He always said I'd find out when I was ready. It stood to reason that, whatever there was to find, was indeed under the egg.

The only problem was that "under the egg" could mean a lot of things—and whatever it meant, I hadn't figured it out. Standing on a chair I'd dragged over, I was still surprised by how much heavier this painting was in my arms than most of Jack's works. For some reason it was painted on wood instead of canvas.

That was just one of the painting's oddities. Another was the frame. Jack rarely framed anything. Usually he sold everything just as he painted it, a canvas on its stretchers. Never with a gilded frame. And while Jack usually worked on a grand scale, sometimes on canvases that almost reached the ceiling, this painting was puny by comparison. Just two or three feet high and not quite as wide. I'm not exactly strapping, but I could manage it fairly easily, and I placed it carefully on the floor against Jack's worktable, still cluttered as he left it with bottles and rags and coffee cans filled with paintbrushes.

I went through the same motions that had as of yet revealed nothing. Flip it around, pore over the back (some faded stamps on the wood, now illegible). Peek around the edges where the painting meets the frame (nada). Inspect the bottom half of the painting, particularly the underside of the frame (nada again).

Next, the mantel. Anything in the bowl, under the actual egg? Nope. Anything under the bowl—either on the underside or sitting on the mantel? Nope. Anything under the mantel? I'd tried to remove the shelf that formed the top, but it was fastened tight. One night I'd used a screwdriver to chip out two or three bricks from the hearth, but only found dark, rotting floorboards beneath.

And so each night ended in a same sense of defeat, the light fading and the shadows settling over the studio.

On that night, I flopped myself down on the floor and contemplated the bare wall above the mantel, wondering if it would be worth busting it open (with what—a drill? a sledgehammer?).

Then a mouse ran up my leg.

Now, I live in an old house in the city. I've seen

my share of mice, even rats. I've seen them on the street, on the subway, even at the playground. But seeing a rodent is one thing. Letting one run up your leg is another.

I jumped, screaming, to my feet, scrambling onto the chair (which was sort of pointless, seeing as how the mouse was already clinging to my leg) and kicking my legs wildly. The last kick sent the little guy leaping for my petticoat, where he dug his claws in some lace trim and held on for dear life. Crazed flapping followed to no effect, so I finally pulled off the skirt, flinging it blindly toward Jack's worktable, where it toppled paintbrushes and bottles of who knows what.

The studio was quiet as I caught my breath and waited for the mouse to emerge from the crumpled skirt. Within seconds I saw his whiskers peeking out of the waistband. "Out!" I shouted, shaking the skirt by the hem, and he bolted, skittering his way over the mess of Jack's table and leaping past the painting still propped below.

The painting! As I looked down, I saw that a bottle of rubbing alcohol had overturned, spilling its contents over the surface, dragging and mixing colors along its path.

I grabbed an old bandanna off the table and

dabbed frantically at the liquid. But the more I rubbed, the more paint I removed, as the rag I held became stormy with a soup of dark colors and the white smears that had once formed the egg.

I crouched there frozen, my hand wavering in midair, my heart sinking as the last connection to my grandfather melted away. As the night's shadows filled the studio, they seemed to pause respectfully just over my shoulder. And as I peered in the dusk, I could just make out—under the paint that was once that everlasting egg—a bird in flight.

Chapter Three

I hadn't slept well since Jack died. The relentless summer heat hadn't helped. Neither had the nighttime creaks and groans of our endlessly complaining house.

Most nights, I lay without even a sheet, tossing and turning with the thoughts I'd held back all day.

What do we eat tomorrow? Will the heat take out all the tomatoes in the garden? Should I go out and water them one more time? If the upstairs toilet goes out again, can I fix it, or will a plumber accept a flat of cabbage as payment?

But tonight I had a new list of questions.

Why would Jack paint over another painting? Was he reusing the canvas and the frame? Or was he hiding it?

What was under there anyway?

Around 3:00 A.M. I got up and took a cold bath in the big claw-foot tub, soaking long enough to cool off, then putting my nightgown back on, sopping wet, and lying in front of the old metal fan. Usually it's enough to get me back to sleep. But not tonight.

At 4:15 the air lifted and ushered in the first light. I headed back up to the studio, armed now with another bottle of rubbing alcohol I'd found in the second-floor bathroom and one of Jack's old T-shirts, wadded in my hand.

The alcohol took off the top layer of paint with alarming ease, and by daybreak most of what had been my last connection to my grandfather was now clinging to the T-shirt rag. I stood back to get a better look in the light.

I pretty much grew up in New York's greatest museums. When other kids were swinging from the monkey bars, I was sitting on the floor of the Met, the Guggenheim, the Whitney, or the MOMA, doodling with my crayons while Jack did his sketching. By the time I was five, I could spot a Picasso, and by eight I knew the difference between a Manet and a Monet.

So yes, I know a Madonna and Child when I see one. The one in front of me had a demure, dark, and big-eyed Mary, sitting with the sleeping Christ

Child on her lap. The child looked about a year old. His outside arm was held open, draped over his mother's leg, and a small bird was flying just out of his grasp—the bird once covered by The Egg.

There was no signature, but along the bottom of the painting was a string of what looked like Latin words, in a single line, reading:

PANIS VITAE / QUI SURREXIT SED NO SURREXIT / PLENISSIMOS NUTRIVIT / ET ANGELUM CURARUM CURAVIT

Within minutes, I'd come to a few conclusions:

It looked old—probably Renaissance, maybe Italian.

It looked real—like something I'd see in a big museum.

It looked like it was worth something—maybe a lot.

Which was strange, because any painting of value from the original Tenpenny collection had been sold a long time ago. Jack had been a painter, not a collector. If there was some image he had admired— a sketch, a study, a scrap torn from a book or magazine—he would have pinned it to the wall for reference, not hidden it from view for the last thirteen years. Maybe—probably—longer.

And this is where I got nervous. Because Jack wasn't just a painter. Not many painters are able to support their families with their art alone, no matter how frugal they are. No, Jack had worked a day job.

As a security guard. At the Metropolitan Museum of Art. In the European Paintings wing.

Which brought me to another conclusion: The painting looked stolen.

As Jack always said, life doesn't stop for lunch, and lunch doesn't stop for life. We still had to eat, so that morning I headed to the garden as usual. I gathered the eggs, pausing to debate whether to still select an Egg of Honor (I did), and pulled the day's haul of pole beans and beets. Beets and beans, of course. Whether fresh or dried, beans made an appearance at every meal except breakfast, with the resulting gastric reverberations. (Jack and I called it "The Ten-penny Symphony.") Beets were even more adaptable. In the summer, grated into salads. In the fall, boiled. In the winter, hot bowls of borscht, and in the spring, when the root cellar was empty and it was too early to plant, there were always pickled beets.

I hate beets.

But today, as I dug and weeded and watered, my daily curses and concerns were pushed aside by a new crop of worries.

What's the punishment for possession of stolen

property? Do they send family members—including thirteen-year-old kids—to jail? What if the kid isn't the one who stole the property? What if the kid just found the property and turns it in? Do they give reward money for stolen paintings? Or do they demand restitution from the thief's family? What if the thief's entire estate adds up to $384 and a fairly reliable flock of chickens?

The sound of a slamming screen door sent the flock fluttering, and a silver beehive hairdo, followed by a pair of manicured hands and two glinting eyes, appeared over the backyard fence.

"What is this?" demanded Madame Dumont, our next-door neighbor and my mother's tea pusher. "Can't you keep these wretched birds quiet?"

Although really it sounded like this:

"Psshhhhh. Wot eez zeess? Cawn't yew keep zese hretched bairds qui-ette?"

Despite fifty years at 20 Spinney Lane, Anne-Marie Dumont still sounded (and acted) as if she'd just arrived from Versailles. According to Jack, Madame Dumont moved in sometime in the 1960s, after he'd sold the adjoining house next door, and it became a boardinghouse. Her complaints started shortly thereafter: His jazz music was unsuitable, his paint fumes were encroaching, and always, the chickens were too loud. Jack was horrified when the boarding-house owner died and left the place to her favorite tenant. Guess who?

"I could not sleep last night with all this noise," Madame Dumont huffed. "All night it was *cocorico* this and *cocorico* that."

"*Coco*—what?" I glanced at the fluffy cluster of coos at my feet. "Do you mean cock-a-doodle-doo? Either way, I very much doubt that since they are all girls, and we've never owned a rooster."

"Nevertheless." This was how Madame Dumont ended all of her arguments. It meant: I may be wrong, but I still won this round.

"Oh, and another thing," she stopped at the screen door and turned back. "I have not received the payment on your mother's account at the tea shop since your grandfather . . . *bof*, how you say . . . passed. Now your grandfather, he has a lot of faults— a rude manner, for one; also, a fast temper and very hogheaded . . ."

"Pigheaded?"

"*Exactement*. And I suspect quite deaf, which seems to run in your family. But," she paused to dab her collarbone with a dainty handkerchief, "he did always pay your bill on time."

"How much is it?" I asked, bracing myself.

"Two hundred fourteen dollars. And seventy-three cents."

I thought I was going to throw up.

"Why? Why on earth did you let my mother charge so much?"

"Ah, I see it is my fault your mother likes the quite rare Asian imports? Nevertheless, she has always paid. That is, until—" She left Jack's death hanging in the air.

"Yes!" I pleaded. "Until that! You know our situation has changed."

"You think you are the only one with difficulties? Bah! I myself was left with nothing and no one else. But I start my own shop, and the only way I keep it so long is to make quite certain all debts are paid. In full."

Leave it to Dumont to use her orphaned poverty to one-up me.

"Listen," I grabbed the fence with both hands, "Madame Dumont, be reasonable. I don't know when—or how—we're going to pay you back. Maybe I could find something—" I looked wildly around for anything I could barter. Apples? Eggs? Beets?

"No. You *will* find a way. Ah," Madame Dumont opened the screen door again, "when you see your mother, remind her the new Golden Assam comes in today."

What? "I just *told* you, we can't afford—"

Slam. Madame Dumont flounced back inside.

Fuming, I delivered my mom's morning oatmeal and tea, ready to lay down an embargo on all future tea purchases. But I was distracted by a photo on her nightstand, a picture of Jack and my mom when she was my age.

"Hey, Mom."

Numbers, symbols, squiggly lines . . .

"Mom!" I tapped her shoulder. "You know that painting in Jack's studio? The one with the egg?"

My mom turned in her seat and looked at me, and a fog momentarily lifted. "Oh, yes, the egg. You know, every morning when I was a little girl, Jack would have me choose the finest egg from the chicken coop, and then we'd place it on a little dish under that painting. And he would always say—"

" 'A new day, a new beginning, a new chance at a new ending.' "

My mother smiled. How long had it been since I'd seen her do that? "Yes, that's it. 'A new chance at a new ending.' "

"So the painting was there when you were a little girl?"

"Yes. Now please," she turned back to her desk, "I was just on the verge of something . . ."

Upstairs in the studio, I looked back and forth between the new discovery and the discolored rectangular space on the wall where the painting had hung for what I now knew was at least forty years.

I worked my way slowly through the tepid oatmeal, but my brain raced ahead.

What if it's some undiscovered work by some famous artist, and wealthy collectors from all over the world flock to buy it, jockeying to outbid each other?

There was something about it that looked weirdly familiar. From my very first glance, I'd felt an almost audible "click" of recognition—but I wasn't able to say why. It was like having an itch that you can't quite find, no matter where you scratch.

I found myself drawn back to the painting throughout the morning, between my chores, returning to sit in its beauty in a house where everything else was falling apart.

Whenever Jack caught me breezing through a museum's galleries, he would practically shout, "Look!

Look! You aren't looking! You're glancing. You're," he said the words as if describing an obscene act, "window-shopping.

"What is the artist trying tell you? There is a message here. Maybe the message is a feeling. Maybe it's a moment in time, or a lens on the world. Or simply the state of being in a single color. But if you look just on the surface, you'll see—what—a portrait, a saint, a myth, a man. But will you see the story? The meaning?"

So I looked. Not just looked, but sat with the painting and drew it in. And the more I looked, the more I saw.

The beautifully modeled faces, the delicate landscape, the sense of a very real knee behind the elegant draping of the Virgin's dress. Together, they all suggested the work of a true master, exactly the kind of thing you'd see in the galleries where Jack worked.

But at the center of that beauty was a kernel of pain and sorrow, like an oyster whose pearl began in the thorny prick of a grain of sand. The composition as a whole carried an unshakable sense of—what was the right word—melancholy? No, straight-up sadness.

Take the Virgin Mary. At first glance, she appeared

peaceful and solid, the anchor around which everything else revolved. But the longer I looked, the more that sense of peace resembled resignation. She held her right hand over her heart, but I couldn't tell if it was a gesture of love or heartache.

The Christ Child—who is almost always painted as an alert and cherubic toddler—here weighed heavily on his mother, his face drawn, his arms slack.

Like a third figure behind the mother and child loomed a small tree, jagged and leafless. And behind the tree, beyond the distant landscape of mountains and lush vegetation, a gathering of dark clouds.

Of course, through all of this, I should've been pickling beets and attending to that upstairs toilet. But by noon, neither the painting nor the chores could keep me in that stifling house.

Mother Nature had draped a wet wool sweater around the city's shoulders that day. On these empty summer days, I had a few options—more limited without hitting my $384 with subway fare. The Jefferson Market Library, usually my first choice, was off-limits until I could find that missing copy of *Franny and Zooey*. There were always the breezes on the piers of the Hudson River Park. Washington Square Park, where I could dip my feet in the fountain. The big modern bookstore with air-conditioning. The clothing stores with air-conditioning, where the security guards would follow me around if I stayed too long.

I walked past a chain store on Sixth Avenue with its doors wide open, its AC spilling out onto the sidewalk. That clinched it. The bookstore would be utterly chilly, and I could sit around as long as I wanted.

That's when the sky finally coughed and unleashed a pelting rain.

When your entire outfit consists of a 1950s nylon slip, your grandfather's old white undershirt, and a training bra made of two handkerchiefs and a piece of elastic you fished out of a pair of sweatpants, you don't really want to get caught in a downpour. So I was running for the bookstore when I heard—

"Hey! Girlie! Get in here!"

I swung around to see Mr. Katsanakis, the owner of New City Diner, holding open the door.

Mr. Katsanakis was not exactly a friend of the family. In fact, he was on my grandfather's list (The League of Nemeses, I called it). Jack had an extensive catalog of personal grievances against most of his acquaintances, stemming from disagreements over art, politics, sports rivalries, money owed (or not owed), parking violations, and garbage can placement. And like a good lieutenant, I accepted Jack's grudges as my own. If Jack knew I was—

"What, you like looking like a wet dog? Get in!"

Dry booths, a discarded *New York Post*, and air-conditioning vs. some long-forgotten slight. I went in.

"You eat already? You hungry?"

What could I say? I had eaten, but I'd been hungry for about a month. I nodded.

"Sit," Mr. Katsanakis growled and tossed a clean dish towel onto the counter. I slid onto a stool and dried off while Mr. Katsanakis located a plate of meat loaf with mashed potatoes and string beans. It was pretty much the last thing you'd want to eat on a humid summer day, but it was all I could do not to grab the food with my bare hands. I hadn't even seen meat in months.

"You eat," he said, and plunked the plate in front of me. Then he sat back and watched me with his hairy arms crossed over his apron, clearly proud of his generosity.

"You eating these days?" he asked.

The question stirred a feeling of disloyalty in me. "Enough," I said, through a mouth full of mashed potatoes.

"Ha!" His laugh was like a rifle shot. "Ha! That's

why you eat like a wolf! A wolf with a meat loaf, ha!"

"Actually, I just ate, thanks." I pushed my plate toward him, with what was probably a visible wince.

"Okay, okay, girlie." He pushed the plate back to me. "You are hard, just like your grandfather. But it does not have to be difficult. You are hungry. I have food. You eat. You come by when you are hungry. Okay?"

"Okay," I mumbled, scruples abandoned in favor of meat loaf again.

"Your grandfather . . ." Mr. Katsanakis sighed heavily. "Jack was a good man. But also a pain in my *popos*."

"I know. He used to say the same thing about you. Except he said *keister*."

Mr. Katsanakis's thick eyebrows lowered threateningly, then popped up again. "Ha! He was right! We are the same that way." He looked at me with tenderness. "We were, I guess." The door jingled with a group of tourists, and he started to move away.

"Um, Mr. Katsa—" I ventured.

"Mr. K, you call me."

"Mr. K then. Just—thanks, I mean."

I was astonished to see him wiggle his eyebrows at me, then wander away, wielding big plastic menus.

I dug back into my feast, feeling happy with just

a side of guilty. As I looked around for a copy of the *Post*, I noticed a girl my age sitting alone at the table behind me.

It was strange to see another girl alone in the city. Jack had given me free rein from the time I was eight, but I might as well have been an orphan. Anytime I went out, someone would stop to ask if I was lost. Even now, other kids my age are almost always in tight groups, arms draped over shoulders, plugged into the same electronic device. "That's the problem with your generation," Jack would say, "letting machines doing the thinking for you."

In fact, the girl at the next table was immersed in her cell phone, too, sometimes jabbing, sometimes swiping, and occasionally even speaking into it. Which is all very well as you sit at a diner, but you wouldn't believe the people stumbling around the sidewalks with their faces glued to these things, not paying attention to a thing around them.

"May I help you?"

I realized I'd been staring this whole time and, naturally, pretended I was studying something utterly fascinating just beyond the girl's head.

"Listen, I don't have any autographs on me, so don't bother asking."

Autograph? So this girl was a famous . . . what? My

knowledge of famous faces was limited to whoever I passed on the newsstand, but this girl didn't look like much of a celebrity. She was wearing a white button-down shirt tucked into high-waisted khaki pants, and her dark, glossy hair was braided in long pigtails, tucked behind each ear. She looked less like a pop star and more like Pocahontas with a job at the Gap.

I let a *psshshh* out of the side of my mouth. "So? Who wants an autograph anyway?"

"Well, I don't do pictures either."

"Well, that's good news, because I don't have a camera."

This struck the girl as very funny. "Oh, okay! Ha. I guess you'll just be getting out your cell phone now. . . ."

"Don't have one of those either."

Now it was the girl's turn to look surprised. "What? How do you text people?"

I shrugged.

"I mean, okay, you can just use e-mail. But what about calls? Do you use pay phones or something?"

I wasn't about to explain that I didn't have anyone to call. I shrugged again.

"Wow, that's cool. Kind of like meeting someone from the olden days who time travels to the future. Like *Return to Tomorrow*, you know?"

"Yeah . . . The book?" I ventured.

"The *book?* No, the movie. Came out last summer? It grossed, like, three hundred mil domestic, seven hundred worldwide. The sequel's in post-production now for release next summer, but you should really download the original first."

"Sure." I understood about three of the words in her last two sentences.

The girl put down her phone and squinted at me. "So you really don't know who I am?"

"Should I?"

The girl smiled, revealing a row of teeth so white and perfect they could only be called dazzling. "Nope, not at all." She got up and joined me at the counter. "I'm Bodhi. What's your name? You live around here?"

"Theo. I live on Spinney Lane."

"Oh yeah? Me too! Just moved in last week."

"Oh, the house with all the—"

"Paparazzi. Yeah. I hate it."

"So your parents are—"

"Jessica Blake and Jake Ford. Yeah."

I was glad she'd filled in the names, because while I might recognize their faces from the newsstand, their names would definitely be pushing the limits of my pop culture knowledge.

"Big house," I said reluctantly. It was the only house on the block bigger than ours. It was also a lot, *lot* nicer.

"It's okay, I guess. They're still moving in and finishing the renovations, so it's too crazy to hang around. I try to stay out all day. This place has become my second home."

"And your parents don't mind?" My experience was the richer the family, the more people watching the kids.

"Who's gonna mind? My mom's in Morocco shooting a new movie. My dad's on set all day in Brooklyn. And we have eight different employees— oh, sorry, I'm supposed to call them 'team members'—anyway, eight other people in the house, all of whom think someone else is watching me." Bodhi looked over to the counter. "Hey, want some pie? On me. Mr. K, two coconut, please!"

First meat loaf, now pie? Yes, please.

Mr. Katsanakis clattered two plates in front of us and went back in the kitchen to yell at the line cooks.

In the space of one rainstorm, I had gone from being one of the Village's eccentric outsiders to being the kind of girl who wanders into her local diner to chat with the owner and share some pie with a buddy.

I kind of liked it.

"Hey," said Bodhi, looking down, "I used to have a pair of sneakers like that! OnDa1 gave them to me—you know, the hip-hop artist? No? He was in a movie with my dad last year. Only got to wear them a couple times before I outgrew them. Where'd you get 'em? I thought the company only made, like, three pairs."

"Hey, I like your . . . shirt." I fumbled for anything to change the subject.

"This?" Bodhi snorted. "This is just my paparazzi uniform. I wear the same thing every day, no matter what. I got the idea from this rock star who used to go jogging in the same outfit every day so the paparazzi's pictures would always look the same. That way they can't sell the pictures, and they leave you alone."

"Aren't you hot, though?"

"Oh, man, I'm sweating my pits out. Why do you think I hang out all day at this diner? AC, baby."

We finished our pie in silence, neither of us able to think of a topic of common interest.

"Why don't we go to your house? Watch TV or something." Bodhi threw some bills on the counter and hopped off her stool.

I hesitated. We hadn't had a visitor in . . . years?

Decades? I'd certainly never had friends over. I didn't even have friends.

Plus there was a certain safety here in the diner, where I existed outside the backyard chickens, the ramshackle house, the strange mother. Couldn't we just stay here? We had pie. We had air-conditioning. What more did we need?

"Hey, let's go." Bodhi already had the door open. "The *America's Got Reality Stars* marathon is coming on."

To my surprise, I found myself saying, "Sure. It's just, we don't have a TV . . ."

And as I left, I wrapped the rest of my pie in a napkin and tucked it in my bag.

Chapter Four

What looked increasingly shabby to me each day looked positively condemned through Bodhi's eyes. I saw the house clearly now: the water stains, the unraveling rugs, the hallways taken over with Jack's hoard of street finds. I rattled on about the house's history and our sidewalk treasures, trying to fill the gaping silence left by Bodhi, whose eyes got wider and wider the deeper we dove.

After a brief tour of the kitchen (puddle under the leaking fridge, mouse droppings under the radiator), I led the way to the garden.

"So . . . this is where we grow most of our food. We don't just go to the grocery store and buy, you know, Chili-Powdered Cheez Janglers, or whatever most people eat. We grow it here. It's a lot better than what you get at the overpriced farmer's market, too.

And the chickens—that's Adelaide, and that little eye-pecker is Artemesia—um, they live over here in the coop. They're pretty quiet. They're all hens, no roosters, you know. But our neighbor," I lowered my voice, "Madame Dumont, she complains all the time that they wake her up in the morning. And that they smell, which you can see, they don't . . ." I stopped, at a loss, and just let the silence settle over the yard.

Bodhi stood rooted, slowly shaking her head. She finally murmured: "This . . . is . . . awesome!"

She walked slowly around the garden, touching the vegetables and tapping at the chickens with her foot. She finally looked up, her face bright with excitement.

"So cool! Seriously. Just phenomenal. I've gotta wrap my head around this. Okay, so . . . do you have a TV?"

"No. Never have."

Bodhi nodded to herself. "So no DVR? No DVDs? No TiVo? Not even a VCR?"

"No."

"Okay, this is fun. What about a dishwasher?"

"Nope."

"Washing machine?"

"Laundromat on Grove Street."

"Okay, don't tell me you don't have a computer?"

"Just the terminals at the library."

Bodhi's eyes narrowed. "What about a bathroom?"

"Yes, of course. Jeez." It was one thing to be thought eccentric but another to be thought unhygienic.

"Okay, okay, had to ask." Bodhi peered around the yard, still looking for an outhouse.

"Seriously. We have two bathrooms. In fact, the one upstairs has one of those old-fashioned toilets where you pull the chain to make it flush."

"Cool! Show me everything! Race you to the top." And before I could stop her, Bodhi was back inside, her footsteps pounding up the stairs.

"What's this room?" I heard from the third-floor landing.

By the time I reached Jack's studio, Bodhi was already riffling through his canvases, pulling out paintings that caught her eye. "I like these," she said, sliding around some wall-sized abstracts. "And I like the colors on this other one. My dad has one like that in his meditation room." She paused momentarily to look up at the painting I'd put back over the fireplace. "But what's that one? Kind of old school compared to the other stuff, isn't it?"

I paused. I thought about how my grandfather had hidden this painting for decades. How he left it to me—and me alone—as a "treasure." How carefully I needed to tread, not knowing what this unpredictable stranger would think or who she would tell.

Blame it on the heat. I spilled it. The paint, the rag, Jack's last words, all of it.

As it turns out, Bodhi was fascinated.

"It's what—a Madonna and Child, you said?" Bodhi pulled out her phone, snapped a few photos, and then started mining Google. "Okay, let's see, search Madonna plus child plus painting plus bird . . . Oh man, twenty million results! Let's try Madonna plus *sleeping* child plus *flying* bird . . ."

"I don't think that's going to help. You could probably find thousands of paintings that fit that description." Impressive words from Jack's art history lessons bubbled up into my mouth. "It's a popular composition of the Renaissance era, perhaps *cinquecento* . . ."

"So, it's what, a family heirloom?"

"I'm not sure. But . . . my grandfather did work at the Met. He was a security guard."

Bodhi's eyebrows went up.

"In European paintings. But he never—"

"Wow. Did he bring home . . . souvenirs?"

"Of course not! You can't sneak anything out. They check your bags; they check your background and references; there are cameras and alarms everywhere." I reached up to pat the painting's elaborate gilt frame. "One time when I was little I put my hands on the frame of a Degas, and a zillion sirens went off. How would you fold up this thing and tuck it in your pocket?"

Bodhi thought for a moment. "I saw this movie once where they cut a painting out of its frame, rolled it up, put it in a suitcase. . . ."

"It's painted on a wood panel," I interrupted, "not canvas. So you could remove the frame maybe, but you'd still have to smuggle the whole thing out."

"Where'd he get it then? And why'd he hide it?" Before I could answer, she finished, "That's the question—well, two questions—isn't it?"

I nodded.

We stood unified before the painting.

"So who painted it?"

"I don't know. But there's something familiar about it . . ."

"What about a signature? What's all this stuff down here?" Bodhi poked her finger at the letters marching along the bottom edge.

"It's not signed. The words are Latin, but I don't know what they mean."

Bodhi was back on her phone. "Well, that's easy enough. Latin-to-English dictionary. We just punch each word in, write it down, and voilà—we have our first clue."

I was liking this. In the five minutes since Bodhi barged in, we'd made more headway together than I had all morning with the painting myself. I grabbed a nearby sketchpad and charcoal pencil, while Bodhi methodically worked her way through the verse. In no time, we had this:

Bread alive, that grew but didn't grow, suckled the plump, and also cured a doctor angel

"Maybe there's a better website," mumbled Bodhi.

Jack was right. This is what you get when you let machines do the thinking for you. "Would you put Picasso into Paint by Numbers? I don't think translation software is the answer here."

"Then you need a translator. Know anyone who just happens to speak fluent Latin? And won't report you and your mysterious discovery to the cops?"

I smiled. "Actually, you just gave me an idea. Wanna come?"

"I guess. Is it really far away? It's brutal out there."

I wrapped a drop cloth around the painting like a present and looked around for something to carry it in.

"I think you'll like it. It's pretty cool."

"I don't know if I'd call this place 'cool.'" Bodhi looked suspiciously around the church sanctuary. "Is someone going to come out and ask me if I love Jesus?"

"You've got to admit it's a lot cooler than my house." And I was right. Stepping into Grace Church was like leaving summer outside and landing in the middle of October. Dark and easily twenty degrees cooler than the street, I was tempted to take off my shoes and chill my bare feet on the marble floor, but thought that might be considered sacrilegious. Or something.

Bodhi was unfazed by such concerns and sprawled out on a pew. "So why are we here? Are you going to confess?"

"No. At least, I don't think so." To be honest, I wasn't sure how this how church thing worked. Always on the lookout for free cultural events, Jack and I had sometimes attended Grace Church's organ concerts, but I'd never entered the building for any spiritual purpose.

As a family, the Tenpennys had been members of Grace Church since 1853—until Jack came along with his committed brand of atheism. Over the years, he'd devised his own worship schedule: Sunday mornings sketching at one of the city's museums, Christmas reading Sartre before the fire, Easter morning working in the garden. I'd followed his lead and never had much need for any church—until now.

But I'd read enough history books to know that priests read Latin. And I'd read enough mystery novels to know that they have to keep whatever you tell them secret.

Just as I was wondering how to summon a priest when you need one, a plump lady in full clerical garb entered the sanctuary from a small door by the altar. She stopped and gave a small bow to the altar, then turned and walked toward the back of the church, her Birkenstocks squeaking up the aisle.

"Hullo there," came a British voice from halfway up the aisle. "May I help you ladies?"

"Um, yes. We're looking for a priest, I guess?"

She came to a stop in front of us and chuckled. "Well, you found one, I guess. Reverend Cecily, you can call me." She shook my hand firmly. "And you are?"

"I'm Theo. Theodora, really. But you can call me Theo."

"Theo-Theodora, welcome." She held my hand in hers warmly. "We are truly happy to have you here."

"Uh, okay, thanks." I withdrew my hand and wondered if Bodhi was right and Reverend Cecily was going to ask if I loved Jesus. "And this is my friend, Bodhi." As soon as I used the word, "friend," I wished I could take it back. But if Bodhi minded, she didn't show it. She just stayed where she was on the pew and gave a little wave.

"Hello there. What a wonderful name, Bodhi. The Sanskrit word for 'enlightenment.' Your parents are Buddhists?"

Bodhi propped herself up on her elbows. "They were when I was born. Or at least their guru was."

"Ah. Well, what can I do for you girls today?" Her eyes dropped to the 1970s blue hardside Samsonite I'd found in the attic, where the painting was zipped neatly into one side.

I moved the suitcase behind my legs. "We're looking for a priest to read some Latin. But you're a . . . I didn't know women—"

"—could be priests? This is an Episcopal church, and indeed they can. And yes, I read Latin. Ancient Greek, too. I studied them for my divinity degree."

Reverend Cecily looked confused. "Do you need homework help?"

"Not exactly."

Reverend Cecily set to work with the painting in her study and sent Bodhi and me to the kitchen to raid the coffee-hour cookies.

"How did you know those words were Latin?" Bodhi asked, her mouth full of Social Tea Biscuits. "Do you take it in school?"

"No, Spanish." I shoved another Nutter Butter in my mouth and slipped three more into the patch-work pockets I'd sewn onto Jack's old T-shirt. "What language do you take?"

"I don't take anything. I'm unschooled."

"What's that?"

"It's kind of like homeschooling but without the school part."

"So . . . it's just . . . being home?"

Bodhi huffed. "No, it's pursuing your own inter-ests, when you want to: Independent study projects, they're called. Like, when my mom was on location in Tanzania, I worked at an animal rescue center, working with baby hippopotamuses. And when my dad did that movie about the inner-city teacher, I wrote a history of hip-hop. And the summer they did that disaster movie together, I pretty much just read all the Tolkein books."

"Oh."

"Whatever. I'm going to school in the city this fall." Bodhi took a swig of apple juice from a paper cup. "Besides, it's not homeschooling when you don't have a home."

"So where did you live before?"

"On sets. On location. In trailers. In hotel rooms. At other actors' houses. Oh, and one year at a Collective Living Experience."

"What's that?"

"Just a bunch of hippies arguing about whose turn it is to do the dishes."

Another cookie in the mouth, another in the pocket. "What about friends?"

Bodhi shrugged. "What about them?"

"Well, how did you make them? Or keep them?" This wasn't just a hypothetical question. I was looking to her for ideas, like a seminar in one of those free flyers around Manhattan: Making and Keeping Friends When You Have Nothing in Common with Your Peers (and Dress Weird).

"Eh, didn't need 'em. I had my mom. I had my dad. Not usually both at the same time. But, y'know,

I had the world. Tanzania! New Zealand! Hollywood movie sets of Tanzania and New Zealand!"

"Sure," I said.

"And there were always people around. Tutors, nannies, assistants, assistants to the assistants. There was always someone to take me where I wanted to go."

"Uh-huh."

The room was filled with the sound of munching cookies.

"But not always someone to go *with*." Bodhi met my eyes again and seemed to search out something there. "Do you know what I mean?"

I knew exactly what she meant. "Yeah. Yeah, I do."

"Ah, there you are, ladies." Reverend Cecily appeared at the door. "Let me fix a cup of tea, and then come to my office. I think I may have solved your mystery."

When we got to Reverend Cecily's office, I saw that the painting was propped on the chair across from the reverend's desk, as if she was offering it counseling.

"Well, a nifty little piece your grandfather picked up here. Where did he get it?"

Reverend Cecily's stream of chatter rescued me from answering. "Now, I don't know much about painting—styles, artists, that sort of thing—but religious iconography I know."

Bodhi perched herself on the corner of Reverend Cecily's desk. "Ico-whattery?"

"It's the symbols," I jumped in. "What they mean, what they're trying to say, sort of like a visual code. Like . . . a skull means mortality. Or a dog means fidelity."

"Or a mirror means vanity. Exactly!" Reverend Cecily clapped her hands again. "You are quite the art scholar."

"My grandfather was a painter."

"He taught you well, I see. Okay, we have ourselves a Madonna and Child, Mary and Jesus, that much you already know. My guess would be Renaissance in style, but to be fair, that's not very realistic. One doesn't find Leonardos rattling around the attic, despite what *Antiques Roadshow* might suggest!" She laughed at her own little joke. "No, I would guess some nineteenth-century painting in the Renaissance style."

"So what does the poem say?" asked Bodhi.

Reverend Cecily picked up a yellow legal pad.

"Now, my background is more church Latin—not poetry—but here we go:

Bread of life
Risen yet unrisen
Nourished the well-fed
And healed the healing angel

"Ummmm, okay. So what does that mean?" interjected Bodhi. I looked over and was surprised to see that Bodhi was staring at the painting intently.

"Well, to be fair, it sounds better in Latin." Reverend Cecily folded her hands over her robes. "But it's basic Christian imagery, really," she started. "In John 6:35, after the Miracle of the Loaves and the Fishes, Jesus says, 'I am the—'"

"'The bread of life,'" I finished, surprising myself. I guess something had sunk in during all those organ concerts.

"Yes! 'He who comes to me will never go hungry.' Spiritual hunger, you understand? Here, he foreshadows the Last Supper. You know the da Vinci painting, of course."

Even Bodhi nodded.

"This is where Christ shared bread and wine with his disciples, asking them to do this again in remembrance of Him after his death. That moment is repeated every week at Mass in what we call Communion. So in calling the Christ Child 'the bread of life,' the painter is alluding to Christ's future sacrifice and to Communion."

"So why is the bread risen but not risen?" I asked.

"It's a—well, not exactly a joke—but a play on words. The Last Supper takes place during Passover, the Jewish festival in which they eat unleavened bread—that is, bread made without any yeast to make it rise. And this painting foreshadows Christ's death, when his life is cut short, but after which he ascends—or rises—into heaven. 'Risen but not risen.' Do you see?"

"And the well nourished? And the healing angel?"

"This one's a bit trickier." Reverend Cecily thought for a moment. "Christ came to offer love to one and all: the rich and the poor, the high and the low. So in this way, He 'nourished the well nourished': his spiritual food fills those who have material wealth but no inner peace. And because He holds dominion over all of heaven and earth, He can comfort even the angels who comfort us."

Reverend Cecily crouched down to inspect the faces further. "While this is nominally a traditional Madonna with the infant Christ Child, I think the painting is really foreshadowing the Last Supper and the end of Christ's life. This isn't the robust toddler you usually see in paintings like these. This Christ Child looks drawn, almost ill, as if He is already filled with suffering. And Mary looks on with such worry, poor dear." The rector clucked her tongue.

"And see this bird? That's the dove, the symbol of the Holy Spirit. See how he descends upon the Mother and Child? That's foreshadowing Christ's baptism, when the Holy Spirit descends from heaven. That's the moment when Christ begins his mission and starts down the path that leads inevitably to his crucifixion."

We all looked closer. You couldn't escape it—the painting was a downer.

"It's a complex painting. Interesting, I think, in the way it imbues a Madonna and Child composition—usually a sweet, peaceful subject—with quite dark undertones."

"So is it worth anything?" Bodhi blurted out.

Reverend Cecily laughed. "That is certainly outside my expertise. But since you're so keen to find out, I know someone who could give you an appraisal. A parishioner of mine works at one of the auction houses uptown. If you bring him the painting, I'm sure he'll be able to ID it in a jiffy." She jotted a name and number down on a slip of paper and handed it to me.

"Thanks, Reverend Cecily. I really appreciate this." I started wrapping up the painting again and settling it back into the Samsonite.

"Not a problem." She glanced at my pockets bulging with Nutter Butters, then she picked up a flyer from her desk and held it out to me. "You know, our church hosts a food pantry, open Tuesday and Thursday mornings. You're welcome to come along anytime."

"Oh. Yeah, thanks. Thanks about the painting." I turned toward the door and left the flyer in her outstretched hand. Jack always said that as long as we had eggs in the henhouse, we didn't need charity.

"Theo, there is one other thing."

"Yes?"

Reverend Cecily hesitated a moment. "It's the 'healing angel' in those verses; I keep coming back to it. Another translation might be 'the angel that heals.'" She walked back over to her desk and opened a large Bible, paging through it until she found what she was looking for. "Here. In the Book of Enoch, we find the archangel Raphael, whose name means 'God heals.' This angel Raphael cures

Tobiah's blindness and brings him safely into the light at the end of his journey."

"Oh?" I waited. "Really?"

Reverend Cecily looked amused. "Why, Theo-Theodora. What would your grandfather say? Doesn't the name Raphael ring a bell?" She laughed at my blank stare. "Raphael the painter? One of the giants of the Italian Renaissance—of painting, full stop?"

Click.

Chapter Five

Raphael. Of course.

In my defense, I'd like to point out that I spent most of that summer in a heat-addled stupor. Also, I suspect that a beet-heavy diet may have deprived my brain of the nutrients needed to recall major artists.

Or maybe I'd been so close to the answer I couldn't see it, the way your name looks like a random jumble of letters if you stare at it too long. Jack loved Raphael and had dragged me to see his work whenever he could: at the Met, of course; on tour at the Frick; even the collection at the National Gallery in D.C., which we'd visited in one day via a round-trip Chinatown bus.

Now a missing part of that collection might be tucked into in my Samsonite, and as Bodhi and I exited through the church's leafy garden courtyard, my brain rapidly sorted through the Raphaels I'd seen, holding them up for comparison.

Bodhi, meanwhile, was halfway down the Information Highway.

"Do you know how much the last Raphael painting went for at auction?" Bodhi practically shouted, staring into her phone.

"Shhhhhh!" I hissed, switching the suitcase from one sweaty hand to the other.

"Thirty-seven million dollars!"

I tripped, almost sending thirty-seven million dollars into a flower bed.

"Hey!" Bodhi dove for the suitcase and caught it just in time. "Careful. You don't want to break your . . . wait . . . got it," Bodhi jabbed and swiped furiously at her phone. "Raphael. Born Raffaello Sanzio da Urbino, actually. Along with Leonardo da Vinci and Michelangelo, one of the Big Three of the Italian Renaissance."

"The three of them pretty much *were* the Renaissance," I launched in. Bodhi might have known movies, music, and hippopotamuses. But I knew art. "Raphael in particular was revered by every future generation of painters, even modernists like Jack."

Bodhi was too focused on her Wikipedia page to

hear me. "Born in 1483, father was court painter to a very powerful duke. He grew up among the elite, and this gave him access to wealthy and powerful patrons when he came of age. Orphaned at eleven and apprenticed out early to famous painters like Perugino." Now she looked up at me. "Know him?"

"Perugino? Sure, the Met has a few of his paintings. Lovely modeling, a real sense of—"

"Raphael moved on to Florence, then on to Rome, where he became the favorite painter of two popes and the Italian aristocracy. Mostly famous for his monumental works across an entire room at the Vatican called the Raphael Rooms, including a painting called—"

"*School of Athens*," I cut in. "His masterpiece, the high point of Humanism, bringing the giants of Classical Greece and Rome into the heart of the Catholic Church."

"Hey, let me get there." Bodhi jumped ahead a few screens. "But Raphael was perhaps best known for—"

My stomach gave a flip. "—his Madonna and Child paintings."

Bodhi glared at me.

"Sorry."

If there was one thing Raphael was famous for,

it was his cuddly Jesuses and adoring Madonnas: seated, standing, alone, with other characters from the Bible. But always lovely and lovable.

Kind of like the one in the very suitcase, now giving me a shoulder cramp.

Kind of. But not exactly.

"Oh, I know these guys." Bodhi was holding up her phone to show me two mischievous angels gazing upward. You'd know them if you saw them, too, a detail from a larger work that has been isolated and reproduced on calendars and greeting cards and chocolate boxes around the world. "So I guess this painting is a big deal, right?"

I took a deep breath. "Listen, we don't know what this is. Like the reverend said, it's probably much later than Raphael. It could be some junky old thing my grandfather found in a pawnshop. It could be some old family heirloom he found down in the cellar and—"

"Then why did he hide it, huh? Explain that!"

I couldn't.

"All right, let's say it *is* a Raphael. That means it's probably," I looked around, "*stolen*. And if it's stolen, no one is giving me thirty-seven anything, except maybe thirty-seven years in the slammer."

We were back on Broadway and stopped to enjoy

the air-conditioning leaking out of a nail salon's doors.

"So what, we drop it in front of the next cop car we see and run?" Bodhi looked disappointed. "This was just starting to get good."

I set the suitcase down and perched myself on top. "Okay, let's think. We have an artist and time period in mind. We've translated the message. What do we need to figure out next?"

Bodhi started counting off on her fingers. "Is it really a Raphael? If not, what is it? Where'd your granddad get it? Why'd he hide it? Why—"

"No, I said *next*. What do we need to know next? Because if it's stolen, we have to turn it in. But if it's just some old painting—well, I could use the money, whatever it's worth. Like, now."

I looked down at the slip of paper Reverend Cecily had handed me. "Let's say we go to this auction house. Worst case scenario: They call the cops. Best case scenario: They say it's mine to keep and it's worth millions."

"Medium case scenario: It's stolen but there's a reward for its safe return?" Bodhi ventured.

"Pretty-good case scenario: It's not stolen, it's not by anyone famous, but it's worth a few thousand, and I sell it."

"Slightly-better-than-terrible case scenario: It's stolen, they haul us down to the precinct, but let us off with a stern warning."

"Highly embarrassing case scenario: It's a Paint by Number kit, and they laugh at us."

"Pretty-unlikely-but-super-dramatic case scenario: They're really vampires, but we fend them off with the Baby Jesus picture, casting them back to the tenth circle of hell."

"Actually, we're already doomed to the tenth circle of hell." I stood up and grabbed the suitcase again. "Because we're about to ride the subway in July."

It was late in the afternoon by the time we got off the subway ($384.00—$2.50 = $381.50) and found Cadwalader's, the Madison Avenue auction house where Reverend Cecily's friend worked. Antique furniture dotted the cavernous modern lobby, a sleek cube of golden marble floors, walls, and ceilings. On the other side of an ocean of Persian carpet sat a polished young man behind a paper-thin computer terminal.

"Yes? May I help you?"

I whispered, "We're not in the Village anymore."

"Upper East Side, all the way," Bodhi whispered back.

"Yes, girls?" He seemed impatient because . . . he had so many other people to wait on? No. As Jack always said: the bigger the desk, the smaller the man.

I strode boldly across the carpet, trailing Bodhi behind me.

"Yes, we're here to see," I double-checked the slip from my pocket, "Augustus Garvey."

"Do you have an appointment?"

I shook my head. "But I am here on," I cleared my throat importantly, "business."

The guy blinked and then said smoothly, "Just a moment. Who may I say is visiting?"

"Theodora Tenpenny."

"And Bodhi Ford." Bodhi poked her head over my shoulder.

"You can tell him just . . . friends of Reverend Cecily."

He blinked again. "Very good. Please have a seat." He gestured to some spindly gilded chairs in the corner.

We tried unsuccessfully to look nonchalant, perched on the edge of the brittle antiques. By the time we heard a sharp clicking sound from the hall, Bodhi had given up and slung her Converse sneakers over my armrest.

We looked up to see a young woman with a long

and well-kept mane teetering on stiletto heels. Her pinched face made me think of an ugly stepsister who regretted borrowing Cinderella's glass slippers.

"Are you the girls here to see Mr. Garvey?"

We scrambled to our feet (which is tough going when your butt has fallen asleep).

"Mr. Garvey has left for the day. I'm Gemma, his associate. Is there something I can help you with?" She hugged a folder to her chest.

I couldn't tell if she had a British accent or was just deliberately pretentious. "Oh, he's not here?"

"Yes, it's Friday. *Everyone* leaves early on summer Fridays," she said with a sniff. This policy did not seem to extend to junior associates.

"Oh, okay. Maybe we should come back Monday—"

"I'm sure Mr. Garvey would want me to," Gemma smiled, "preview anything you've brought."

Bodhi and I exchanged a glance. Bodhi shrugged "why not?"

As I opened the suitcase, I explained the strange discovery of the painting, conveniently leaving out Jack's place of employment. Bodhi helped me prop the frame on a chair, where it looked no more at ease than we did.

"The poem says—"

"Yes, I know, I read Latin," Gemma said shortly.

We stood by silently as Gemma put her face up to the painting, stood back several paces, donned a pair of white cotton gloves she fished out of her blazer pocket, and then turned the frame around to inspect the back. She placed the frame neatly back against the chair and began pulling off the gloves, one finger at a time.

"Well, girls, thank you for bringing it in. It is quite an interesting painting." She offered up her pinched smile again.

We all looked at each other. "And?" I probed.

The smile disappeared. "And it is difficult to definitively determine the period, let alone the artist."

Bodhi hooked her thumb at me. "She thinks it's a Raphael."

I was starting to wonder if Bodhi was a help or a liability.

"A Raphael? Well, well, well, you've been doing your homework, I see. No, dear, I don't think it's a . . ." she stopped here to smirk, "Raphael. First of all, the complete *oeuvre* of Raphael is very well documented, and the likelihood that you just stumbled across an undiscovered work is, well, optimistic, don't you think?"

"I guess," I conceded.

Gemma was warming to her own expert opinion. "Look at the Christ Child, for example. Wan, thin, bearing no resemblance whatever to the warm, rounded hallmarks of a Raphael infant.

"And even if it were a 'Raphael,'" here Gemma used air quotes, a habit I decided now to despise forever, "it could still *not* be a Raphael. It could be Circle of Raphael, Follower of Raphael, Workshop of Raphael, School of Raphael, After Raphael . . ."

Yep, I thought, deliberately pretentious.

"I suppose it's possible it's a *pastiche*, a copy by a student or an admirer. Not necessarily a *talented* admirer," Gemma tossed her golden locks behind her ear. "The panel and frame do look authentically old, certainly as early as seventeenth century, possibly *cinquecento*."

"So it could be a contemporary, a student?" I ventured. "Wouldn't that be worth something?"

Another smirk.

"I think in this case, there's another consideration. That it's a fake. Getting an old but not terribly valuable canvas and painting over it—it's an old trick forgers use to feign authenticity."

I stared at the surface, straining to see underneath this layer of paint to another lurking below.

"Okay, so how do you establish really authentic authenticity?"

"Here at Cadwalader's, we have a wealth of tools at our disposal. There's microscopic analysis of the *craquelure*—that is, the depth of the lines that develop in the dried paint. We analyze paint pigments to see if the minerals therein are contemporary with the artist in question. We can do carbon dating on the frame and canvas. We can even use infrared and X-ray technology to reveal the original drawings or painting underneath the top layers."

Bodhi's eyes lit up. "X-ray? Yeah, let's see what's under there!"

Gemma glanced at her watch. "Listen, this isn't a children's museum. We don't undertake these costly experiments just to 'see what's under there.'" Again with the air quotes. "We would be inclined to investigate further *if* we thought there was reason to believe . . . But in this case," Gemma's eyes flicked over me from threadbare T-shirt to hip-hop sneakers.

"Not to be blunt, but I take it your family has some . . . financial concerns? Isn't it possible your grandfather created this painting with the intention of fooling a less-discerning auction house?"

Another look at the watch. Probably trying to make an early train out to the Hamptons.

"No," I said, holding Gemma's eye and raising my voice. "That is not possible. My grandfather was not that kind of man." But as my voice echoed back to me in that lobby-mausoleum, I realized I didn't know my grandfather any better than Gemma did. Just a month ago, I would have called Jack the dictionary definition of integrity. But holes kept appearing in that façade, and an alternate story kept dribbling in.

"Well, you are welcome to get a second opinion at another auction house. There's always Sotheby's, Christie's, and a myriad of smaller houses. But I do thank you for bringing the painting in. It has provided a welcome Friday afternoon diversion."

And with just a few clicks, Gemma was gone.

"So that's that?" grumbled Bodhi as we stood waiting for the 6 train (down to $379.00). The platform felt even hotter after the brittle chill of the Cadwalader's lobby. I still don't understand how my cellar stays dry and cool all summer, but the subway platforms manage to be even hotter and steamier than the sidewalk above.

I peered down the tunnel, telepathically willing the train to arrive. "I guess so. But—"

"I wanted to punch her. Reminded me of these assistants on set, with their stupid headsets and clipboards. Everyone hates them. I bet everyone hates Gemma." Bodhi let the name drop out of her mouth like chewed gum.

"But something she said makes no sense."

"A lot of what she said made no sense. *Pastiche. Cinquecento. Gemma.* Ugh."

"No, listen." I bit my thumbnail. "Why would you create a fake Old Master by painting over an old canvas, and *then* paint over it again?"

"Beats me." Bodhi kicked an empty soda can onto the subway tracks, sending a rat scampering.

"Seriously. If my grandfather wanted to fake a painting and cash in on it, wouldn't he just go out and try to sell it? Why would you fake a painting and then hide it for—what, forty, fifty years?"

"That's true," nodded Bodhi.

"And there's something else I don't understand. Why did that rubbing alcohol take off the top layer of paint, but not the bottom layer? *That* doesn't make any sense. If it's the same paint, why wouldn't it have the same effect on both layers?"

"Hmmm. That's a good question, actually." Bodhi perked up a little. "Does this mean that the mystery's still on?"

"You could say that." I peeled my T-shirt away from my chest and flapped it back and forth. "But listen,

I'm tired of these so-called experts. They don't have the answers anymore than we do. That Gemma—"

"Gemma," Bodhi spat out.

"She barely looked at the thing."

"And Reverend Cecily—well, she's a nice lady and everything, but she had her own . . . prejudice, you know?"

"Preconceived notions, you mean. And yeah, I know."

A hot wind blew at our ankles, signaling the 6 train.

"Jack never did anything without a very good reason. And I want to know the reason behind," I nudged the suitcase with my sneaker, "this. We need to become our own experts." I fumbled suddenly. I still wasn't convinced that this should be a group project. "I mean, *I* need to do more research. Read more, look at more paintings, learn more about how paint works, stuff like that. I think I'll hit the library as soon as they open tomorrow morning."

"Cool! I'll come over beforehand and help feed the chickens."

"Really?" Was it possible Bodhi really wanted to hang out with me? Or was she just looking for another "independent study project"? "I mean, okay. I guess."

"I need to get out of the house anyway," Bodhi shouted over the rush of the barreling train. "*People* magazine is coming over to do a feature on my dad's yoga room. I don't want to spend the day watching him do the Flying Crow."

Chapter Six

I hadn't expected to chase Raphaels all afternoon. By the time I got home, it was clear the house was feeling neglected and was going to take it out on me— starting right with the front door, which dumped its heavy brass doorknob into my hand. The upstairs toilet swirled spitefully. My mother "helped out" by dumping her dirty laundry on the hallway floor.

The garden was paying the heaviest price for my extracurricular activities: stems drooped, vegetables shriveled in the heat. Love your garden, and it will love you back, as Jack would say. Same goes for chickens. But today the chickens were peeved too, and Artemesia pecked my foot when I scattered some chopped beet greens as a guilt gift.

I spent the next morning atoning, and by the time I stopped for breakfast, I had redrilled and replaced the stripped screws on the front door, accosted the upstairs toilet, cleaned out the chicken coops, and turned the compost heap.

The timing of those last two items is not coincidental. The key to a good garden is, of course, good compost. What makes good compost? A secret ingredient: chicken poop. Trust me, when you bite into a juicy tomato or succulent squash, it's chicken poop you have to thank.

Anyway, those chores alone took me through a late breakfast. I had just brought up my mother's tray ("What, no Irish Breakfast?"), when I heard a rap from the big brass knocker on the front door.

"Hi!" shouted Bodhi, already sweating through her anti-paparazzi uniform. "Too early?"

"Well, I've still got a lot to finish up around here. I was just about to start some pickling." I looked skeptically at Bodhi. "Do you want to help?"

Bodhi's face shone. "Sure, sounds great! Like *Little House on the Prairie.*" She bounded her way into the parlor. "I did an independent study project on Laura Ingalls Wilder when I was eight, back when we were at the Collective Living Experience. A couple of the guys even helped me build a log cabin. But then they all got into some argument about privatized property, and we moved back to Malibu."

With Jack around, the morning chores had felt like a well-oiled machine, and now without him, a clanky one running on fumes. But something about Bodhi's enthusiasm made the whole operation feel . . . well, fun. "Got any music?" she asked, so I found a Benny Goodman record for the parlor phonograph, cranked it up, and led Bodhi down the stairs to the kitchen, where I'd already lined up Mason jars, canning racks, and tongs. Beets and a few cucumbers stood at the ready, washed in colanders in the big farmhouse sink, while every soup pot, stockpot, and lobster pot had been rounded up, filled with boiling water on the stove.

I showed Bodhi how to fill the jars with the veggies, vinegar, and spices and was surprised by how easily she jumped in, dancing around to "Sing Sing Sing (With a Swing)" as she worked. Most of the girls from school would balk at something so domestic—even dorky—on a summer morning. But a couple of hours later, the jars were cooling, and we'd moved on to the garden, pulling weeds and slapping mosquitoes with our beet-stained fingers.

"It's funny," said Bodhi as she tossed a dandelion she'd pulled to the chickens. "They all have their own personalities, don't they? Like this one." Bodhi rubbed the side of a silkie bantam with the toe of her sneaker. "She's a little softy. Just wants a cuddle."

I put down the basket of eggs I'd collected and picked up Adelaide, who was nuzzling my shoe.

"That's Frida. Her sister, Adelaide, here is the same way. You can pick her up if you want. Just support her feet, like this." I gave her head a little scratch and Adelaide clucked appreciatively. "But look out for Artemesia, that frizzy one over there. She'll go at you if you get too close." Artemesia flapped her wings theatrically, and Bodhi pelted her with a dandelion.

"What's with the funny names?" asked Bodhi.

"All famous artists. All women. A little joke I had with my grandfather."

Bodhi knelt down to stroke the hen who'd been diligently working on a hole next to the coop. "Who's this little digger?"

"Theodora," I mumbled.

"Theodora? What artist is that? Or—wait, you named the chicken after yourself?"

It had been last summer, the day Jack brought out two new chicks he'd gotten from his breeder in Bed-Stuy. The chicks were now big enough to join the flock, and one—quickly named Artemesia—asserted her claim on the feed right away. Some of the older, wiser chickens squawked and flapped at her, schooling her on the pecking order, but Artemesia squawked back, and soon we had a real feather-flier on our hands. It took us ten minutes to get everyone back to their corners.

But when the feathers settled, we looked down and saw that most of the feed was gone. Nearby, the other new chick had her head down and kept scratch, scratch, scratching, determined to find more food.

"Ha! See that one? She let the others flap and fight and fuss at each other, while she kept her eye on the prize. Smart girl, just like you," Jack had said. "Let's name her Theodora."

"Gee, thanks. Why not Angelika? Or how about Little Jackie? That has a nice ring to it."

"Well, she's not a rooster, so Jackie doesn't make sense." Jack pulled a lock of my hair. "And Angelika—well, your mom's a songbird at heart. She just keeps flying overhead, circling and circling and never landing on anything."

On that particular day, I had had to decline a rare birthday party invitation from a girl in my class whose mother had insisted she invite everyone. We couldn't afford the cost of the train out to her weekend house, let alone an appropriate gift.

"Who ever said I wanted to be a chicken?" I groused. "Maybe *I'd* like to be a songbird. Maybe I'd like to fly away somewhere for once."

There was a very long pause, and when I looked up at my grandfather, I was surprised to see that his hands were in his pockets and his eyes were glassy.

"Why do you think we've hung on to this house?" he asked, his voice low. "Don't you know I could cash out and give it over to the yuppies who would polish it up like a Fabergé egg? The reason we stay—the reason my father stayed, and his father stayed, and his father stayed—is that this house is ours. This city is ours. Never let anyone tell you any different. Because, if you don't dig in, trust me—they'll dig you out."

Jack picked up Theodora the Younger and stroked the top of her head.

"One day I'll pass on—and don't get any ideas, sister, the doctor says I've got the body of a man twenty years younger."

"I know, I know, you keep telling me—"

"One day I'll pass on, and this house will be yours. This house and everything in it. It's the only legacy I can offer you. But it will also be your burden to shoulder—to finish the work that I couldn't."

At the time, I had assumed that burden was my

mother. Jack's expectations had always been clear: That I would take care of my mom the same way he dropped out of school to support his own mother through the Depression.

But it was only now, on this morning out in the garden with Bodhi, that I remembered those words and wondered if the painting was the burden Jack intended. Or the legacy. Or both.

I was jarred back to the moment by the familiar thwack of Madame Dumont's screen door. As expected, two eyes and a beehive appeared over the wooden fence. Jack always regretted that he'd made that fence too short.

"Oh, good, Theodora," she launched in without a glance Bodhi's way, "I need to speak with you. *Alors,* your mother's debt is now to two hundred and twenty-nine dollars—"

My mouth gaped open but no words came out. "What?" I finally sputtered. "Why? I told my mom to stop going to the tea shop. I told you to stop selling her tea!"

"She never had the Smoked Oolong. It has a certain *je ne sais quoi.*" Yes, we get it, Madame Dumont. You're French. "This is becoming very serious, you see? I would hate to—*comment dit-on?*—to retain counsel."

My head was spinning. "Counsel? What's counsel?"

"A lawyer," she replied icily. "And when I speak to this lawyer, I will also ask about the city noise regulations. For your roosters."

"For the last time!" I exploded, embarrassed at the unhinged screeching in my ears but too angry to stop myself. "We don't have any roosters! We have *never* had roosters! For fifty, sixty, maybe even two hundred years, we have not had roosters! For the love of Pete, roosters *do. not. lay*—"

An object sailed over my head, a white object that glinted in the morning sun and traveled a perfect arc that led straight to Madame Dumont's head.

Now Madame Dumont was the one who sounded unhinged, shrieking as she tried unsuccessfully to shake eggshell and egg whites out of her helmet of hair, all the while dodging the new missiles Bodhi lobbed her way.

She let fly a string of French not found in a school textbook, pausing long enough to pronounce us: "Wicked, wicked girls! I will take this to my lawyer. No, to the police! I will! You wait and see!" Madame Dumont's screen door slammed closed again.

"Who was that anyway?" Bodhi turned to me, lightly tossing the last egg back and forth between her hands. "Kind of a cranky old baguette, right?"

Frozen in place, I stood stunned and staring at that last egg in Bodhi's hand.

"You okay?"

I tried to take some deep breaths, then began to heave gasps of air, my body shaking as I sank slowly to my knees and fell back, right in the middle of the pecking flock.

"Oh, man." Bodhi plopped down next to me and threw her arm around my shoulders. "Oh jeez, I'm sorry, Theo. I'll buy you more eggs. I'll buy you a dozen. I'll buy you a whole bunch of omelettes. I just couldn't help myself." She thought for a moment. "I have kind of a problem with impulse control. At least that's what my mom's shrink says."

But what Bodhi didn't realize is that great guffaws welling up from my belly were sobs mixed with laughter, dislodging that pit of knots I'd lived with for the last month—for the last thirteen years, if I was honest. I was shocked at Bodhi's sheer nerve; I was laughing at what Jack would think to see it; I was crying that he never would—and yes, I was mourning the loss of the eggs, too. And as I allowed myself to rest my head on Bodhi's shoulder—imagine that, on a friend's shoulder—I laughed and cried to think that I actually had someone to lean on.

I wiped my sweaty, teary face on my sleeve. "I've

always wanted to do it. But I could never spare the eggs."

Bodhi held up the egg in her palm. "There's one left. You still have a chance."

I stood up and helped Bodhi up, too. "No. I know a better place for that egg. And you've earned the right to put it there."

After a lunch of tomatoes, peppers, and one shared scrambled egg (we used the Egg of Honor we replaced with Bodhi's more heroic one), we escaped the heat of the house at the Jefferson Market Library.

I hadn't been to the library since the day Jack died, and while I mourned the loss of my grandfather, the library came in a close second.

The public library is the closest I'll ever come to a shopping spree. Once, twice, sometimes three times a week, I'll drop in, raid the stacks, wielding my library card like a socialite with a Bloomingdale's charge account. I grab anything that looks interesting, flipping through a few pages before losing interest or devouring the whole thing in one sitting. And if I don't like it, I can return it. It's the only place where I can be wasteful with no consequences.

As long as I return the books on time.

The day Jack died was also the day *Franny and*

Zooey went missing. A missing book meant not only late fines, but a replacement fee. That was a hit I couldn't afford on $384—wait, $379. Every time I walked by the Jefferson Market branch, I could practically feel Ms. Costello, the ancient librarian, suspending the missing book over me with her liver-spotted hand.

But now we needed the full catalog of the New York Public Library at our disposal. So I gathered up my entire collection of outstanding books—even the ones I hadn't cracked yet—and hauled them back to the returns desk as a peace offering.

I can't remember the first day Jack brought me to the Jefferson Market Library; we were always just drawn there. "Now, this is my church," Jack would say as we mounted the deliciously gloomy Gothic tower toward the stained-glass windows above. He always stopped to read "his creed" carved at the top of the stairway: "The precepts of the law are these: to live correctly, to do an injury to none, and to render to every one his own"—a holdover from the building's original function as a jail and courthouse.

Today Ms. Costello wasn't at her usual perch, so we dumped my books in one of those anonymous returns boxes and went straight to the Information Desk. There we found a beefy . . . well, dude, for lack of a better word. With a shaved head, old-timey moustache, and a spiral of tattoos disappearing up his shirtsleeve, he whistled as he zipped around his desk, propelling his wheeled office chair with his shiny two-tone wingtips.

Bodhi murmured, "Did the library hire a bouncer?" I shrugged. Sure, the library attracted its share of oddballs, but it wasn't like a biker bar or anything.

The desk chair stopped mid-slalom. "Whoa! How long have you been standing there?" His voice did not suggest that we were in a library. "What can I do you for?"

"What happened to Ms. Costello?"

"Well, they say she retired, but if you ask me, I think she ran off with Vincenzo the janitor, because he quit the same day." He winked. "Just a hypothesis, though."

"Are you . . . a librarian?"

"Sure am. I'm Eddie." He reached out over the desk and shook our hands forcefully. "Freshly minted MLIS and at your service."

"Nice tattoo." Bodhi pointed to the baroque symbol on his wrist.

"Thanks!" Eddie's volume dial seemed stuck at eleven. "That's my band's logo. We play thrash ska on Tuesday nights at the Snake Pit. It's sick! You guys should come—wait, you aren't twenty-one, are you?"

We shook our heads.

"Never mind. Anyway, what are you guys looking for today?"

"We're doing a project," I said.

"For school," chimed in Bodhi.

"Yeah, summer school." I pulled out my notebook. "We need to get books on—let's see here . . ." I glanced at Eddie. "You ready?"

Eddie smiled and positioned his hands at the computer terminal like a virtuoso. "Ready."

"Okay, we need books on the Italian Renaissance in general, probably the Northern Renaissance too—Flemish, German, Dutch . . ."

". . . German, Dutch, got it . . ." Eddie's fingers flew over the keyboard.

"Specifically books on Raphael, both biographies and monographs. Also books on art fakes and forgeries, stolen art . . ."

Bodhi poked me. "Rubbing alcohol."

"Oh yeah, something on, I guess, paint chemistry? Or how paint works? Or dries?"

". . . Paint chemistry . . ." Eddie repeated and peered into the computer. "Okay. Are you ready for

a Dewey decimal avalanche?" He hit print and unleashed a sheaf of paper our way.

"All righty! Take that, summer school!" Eddie got
way more pleasure out of the online catalog than
any librarian I'd ever seen. "You'll need a shelving
cart just to get that to the circulation desk!"

"Oh." I'd almost forgotten. "But there's one problem . . . It's a book. A library book. I can't find it
anywhere—"

"Gimme your card," interrupted Eddie.

I placed my library card on the desk and watched
him swipe and scroll. "It's *Franny and Zooey*. I know I
had it, but. I've looked and looked . . ."

"Whoa, you're one of our frequent fliers!" he ob-
served, glancing through my record. "I should've
guessed."

"Yes, see, I'm here all the time. I've never had so
much as a late fee—we can't really afford late fees—
but even if we could, I'm very diligent about—"

Eddie jabbed the keyboard commandingly a few
times and hit return. "Done. The New York Public
Library system has absolved you of your sins." He
made some semi-magical signs in the air.

"That's it?"

"That's it." Eddie winked again. "Just make sure

these don't go disappearing. Now, what's next? Modern animatronics? History of the hot dog?"

"No, I think we've got everything." I started to gather up the stack with its columns of call numbers. "So, you are sort of a research . . . specialist, right?"

"You got it. MLIS, Master's of Library and Information Science—with an emphasis on information."

"Do you know anything about military records?"

"Not much myself, but let me introduce you to my dear friend, Google." Eddie was back at the keyboard again. "You want to find someone's record?"

"My grandfather's." I pulled the Veteran's Affairs letter out of my bag and handed it to Eddie. With the discovery of the painting, I wasn't willing to leave any questions floating around unanswered.

Eddie tickled his keyboard some more, referring to the letter here and there. "Okay, here's his draft record."

"What, just like that?"

Eddie grinned. "Just like that. See for yourself." Bodhi and I leaned over the desk. "There's the serial number, there's where he enlisted—here in New York, right after Pearl Harbor—see, December 11, 1941. He was eighteen years old; occupation: artist; and he lived in New York. Class: Private."

"So he served in the army?" This was news to me. "Where did he go? Did he fight?"

"Doesn't say. This is just the draft record, which tells us he enlisted but doesn't say which division he got assigned to. For that, you have to submit an application to the National Archives." Eddie jumped ahead a few screens. "You can do it all online. There's just a twenty-dollar fee."

My heart sank. Twenty dollars meant a week's worth of groceries, or keeping the lights (and fans) on for another week, or a dent in my mom's mounting bill at the tea shop—not the beginning of a wild-goose chase.

Another card hit the desk, but this one was shiny and silver. ("Platinum," Bodhi would later call it.) "Let's do it," Bodhi said.

Eddie looked skeptical. "Your parents okay with this?" He glanced at me. "Are *you* okay with this?"

If there is one thing that Jack always told me, it's that Tenpennys pay their way. Tenpennys owe nothing to anyone. Tenpennys do it themselves or do without.

"Yes," I said decisively. "Thank you," I mouthed to Bodhi.

Bodhi shrugged and slid the card across the table to Eddie. "So, how long to get the records?"

Eddie checked the website again. "Anywhere from ten days to six months."

I groaned. "Six months?"

"Don't worry," Bodhi patted my back consolingly. "It'll take you that long just to read all these books."

Chapter Seven

Bodhi's mom wanted her to fly out to Morocco and meet some Sufi mystic-to-the-stars, so Bodhi headed off for two weeks with a laptop under her arm. "I'll handle the Internet research," she said the next morning as she headed for the airport, her head poking out of the taxi's window. "I'll have a lot of downtime once our camel caravan gets to the monastery. They have Wi-Fi and a pool."

That was fine with me. The minute Bodhi saw the stack of books on my reading list, she took care to inform me that she was "more of a kinesthetic learner." And frankly, as much as I loved the library, the less time I had to spend around the creepy guys at the computer terminals, the better.

No, I would spend the following week where I felt most at home: alone with my books and my paintings. After my morning chores, I'd walk the length of the island to the Met or the Frick, exploiting their pay-as-you-wish policies to trade a penny for a few hours with their Renaissance collections. In the late afternoons, I hunkered down in Jack's studio, sweating over the reading, paging damp fingers through biographies and histories and the For Reference Only monograph Eddie let me smuggle out: three-hundred-some pages of every painting, sketch, and poem to ever leave Raphael's hand.

When I wasn't reading, I was looking, just like Jack always told me. For a man who found something (or someone) to complain about wherever he went, you would be surprised how much Jack looked for beauty in the world. It was like an effort of forced optimism in the face of his own cantankery. He'd stop me in the middle of the street to check out the filigree work of a manhole cover or call me up to his studio to watch the golden-pink sunlight settle over Wall Street's towers. "If you stop and look," he once told me as we gazed at a fireworks display of cherry blossoms on East 11th Street, "you will be amazed at what you find."

So I spent those two weeks really looking. I looked at Michelangelos and Leonardos, of course, but also Peruginos, Bellinis, Titians, Georgiones, Simibaldos,

Lottos, Pintoricchios, Solarios, Tifernates, Botticellis, Ghirlandaios, and all the Fras (Fra Bartolommeo, Fra Filippo Lippi, Fra Lippo Lippi, Fra Angelico).

And the more I looked, the more the painting in Jack's studio looked like a Raphael.

But this was a problem in and of itself. For one thing, the more likely it was a Raphael, the more likely it was stolen.

Still, if there was one thing I'd learned from the books on art fakes that Eddie found for me, it was that the best way to "find" an Old Master painting is to really, really want to find one.

For example, there was this guy in 1940s Holland who specialized in forging Vermeers. Everyone wants to find a Vermeer—there are only about thirty-five known canvases in the world, and each one is worth a fortune. So experts fell all over each other to authenticate this one fake religious painting—even though it was a subject Vermeer never painted, in a size he never painted, and in a style that looked *nothing* like his other paintings! But everyone wanted to discover a Vermeer, so a Vermeer it became. For a while, at least.

I had to focus on the hard facts, like when Raphael might have painted this particular Madonna and Child. So when the light faded in the studio each night, I headed down to the kitchen and strained my eyes to read one more book. It was one recommended by Eddie, who had called it "a backstage pass to the Italian Renaissance": *The Lives of the Most Excellent Painters, Sculptors, and Architects* by an artist named Giorgio Vasari.

Imagine for a minute that you attend Great Painters of the Italian Renaissance High School. Like any high school, you have cliques, rivalries, and big personalities. Vasari is the school gossip. Vying for valedictorian you've got Leonardo da Vinci, the quirky supernerd, and Michelangelo, the angry but brilliant loner. Then you have the guy everyone wants to be seen with: the star quarterback who's been elected both Class President and Most Popular.

That's Raphael.

You could also add "Class Flirt" to his list of titles. According to Vasari, Raphael was a "very amorous person, delighting much in women." He strung along an engagement to the niece of a powerful cardinal for seven years while he fooled around with his mistress, even refusing to finish the Pope's frescoes unless she was brought to his villa for "inspiration." Vasari records his early death at thirty-seven as due to "sexual excess"—a medical condition that I'm pretty sure has since been disproven.

This true love of Raphael's, a local girl named Margherita Luti—nicknamed "La Fornarina" or the "Baker's Daughter"—pops up throughout his work. Raphael adored the plump brunette and used her again and again as a model. Many of those famous Madonnas are based on her.

He painted her portrait, too: once as an elegant woman in sumptuous robes and a modest veil (*La Velata*) and once in a pose better suited for a girlie magazine, topless except for a transparent wisp held coyly to her chest.

Now some scholars deny these two paintings are of the same woman. Some even say that La Fornarina was a myth. But Renaissance artists loved nothing more than to leave little clues and riddles in their paintings, and Raphael was no different. So put the portraits side by side and look for yourself. Why are the women in the exact same pose: half profile, their right hand held lightly to their left breast? Why do they have the same almond-shaped dark eyes, the same Roman nose, the same full lips and dimpled chin?

And why did he add a dangling pearl ornament in the exact same place on each woman?

Because the Latin word for pearl is *margarita.*

Margherita. As in Margherita Luti, La Fornarina.

Which brings us back to the painting upstairs in the studio. Big-eyed beauty? Check. Right hand also held to her left breast? Check. Pearl in hair? Check. I held my breath as I put down the monograph: the resemblance was undeniable. There was just one question. Why was the Madonna in my painting so forlorn and Raphael's Fornarina always so radiant?

A few days later, I found a slip of paper under my front door from Bodhi: "K's diner, 10:00 A.M.? PS: Get a cell phone."

Bodhi was back. It was time to compare notes.

I grabbed a few of the most relevant library books, ready to debate the finer points of the School of Raphael vs. Style After Raphael. But there was one puzzle I hadn't been able to crack: the paint itself.

I was still stumped by why the rubbing alcohol had removed the top layer of paint while leaving the bottom intact. I'd been dipping in and out of a book called *The Chemistry of Paint and Materials for Working Artists.* But I could never get more than a few pages in without admitting defeat. Seventh-grade biology hadn't given me much of a basis for advanced chemistry.

At ten minutes to, I left the house, the books straining my sweater bag and my eyes glued to *The*

Chemistry of Paint (with the occasional glance at the sidewalk to avoid stepping in anything).

"Look out, miss. This is how you are going to get hit by a car."

Without looking up, the scent of roasted vanilla told me I had reached Sanjiv's Toasty Nuts cart.

"You want the toasty nuts today? Cashews are very good today."

The smell, so seductive on a cold winter's day, was overpowering when it mingled with the smell of smog and urine rising from the hot sidewalk. Despite my hunger, I shook my head.

Sanjiv sighed. "Yes. No one wants the toasty nuts in the summer. In Mumbai it would not make a difference. In Mumbai I would be reaching for my—"

"Yes, reaching for your sweater, I know." I smiled kindly as I cut him off. Some days, this little joke accounted for my only human interaction, even though Sanjiv had been on Jack's list, something involving permits and the legally restricted vendor space on the sidewalk. But since Jack died, this small exchange had become something I looked forward to, despite—or maybe because of—its predictability.

But today I had a mission and, what's more, a real, live friend waiting for me.

"Yes, you have heard this one." Sanjiv sighed again.

"Well," my eyes automatically went back to my book as my feet started moving again, "stay cool, Sanjiv."

"Ah, I see you are now a chemist like me."

"What?" I stopped.

Sanjiv pointed at the book. "You read about chemistry? This is what I teach, back in India. At my school, you know?" He gestured at the picture next to the empty coffee can marked DONATIONS PLEASE, where Toasty Nuts customers were encouraged to drop a few coins for the school where Sanjiv once taught. Twelve or so high school kids were posed around a single Bunsen burner, proudly wearing the safety goggles Sanjiv had sent them.

"Oh yeah, that's right. Maybe you could explain some of this to me." I handed him the book. "But it's about paint chemistry, so—"

"Yes, paint, I know about paint. Before I became a teacher, I worked in a lab in a big chemical company. They made roof coating, waterproofing materials, paint . . ."

"Are you serious?"

"Yes, I am serious. Why would I joke about this?" Sanjiv looked confused.

"So you know about oil paint, for example?"

His laugh was almost a sneer. "Yes, miss, I know

about oil paint. This is a very important kind of paint! But I want to know—what do *you* know about oil paint?" He handed me back the book.

I told Sanjiv about the painting: the rubbing alcohol, the top layer coming off in strips, the bottom layer pristine. "So what I can't figure out is why the alcohol removed one layer but not the other."

"Okay, this is easy. You say your grandfather painted over the first painting? That is why the top layer came off. This top layer was young. It was painted later."

He scooped a few cashews into a small paper bag and handed it to me. "The bottom paint was much older. It would have to be very old if your rubbing alcohol did not harm it."

I nodded, chewing slowly on the cashews. "My grandfather used to say that the best thing about oil paints is that they took a long time to dry. So he could work on a painting slowly and change things over time."

"Not dry, no." Sanjiv wagged his finger at me. "Oil paint does not dry. It reacts with the oxygen in the air and hardens. 'Polymerize' is the word in English, I think. But your grandfather was right, it takes a very, very long time before the paint is hard enough to resist a solvent like turpentine or rubbing alcohol."

"How long?"

"Maybe one hundred years?"

My voice shook slightly with excitement. "So if you rub alcohol on some—let's say—forty- or fifty-year-old oil paint, it will just come off, right?"

"Eh, this I am not so sure." Sanjiv rubbed his smooth chin as if searching for a beard. "It would smudge, yes, but wipe off so easy? I do not know about this."

We stood thinking, over the steaming sweet cart, sweat droplets trickling down our temples as if we squeezed them out with our brain power.

"But maybe your grandfather uses another kind of paint: maybe acrylic, maybe something else. Something that is not so stable as oil paint."

Something engineered to be easy to remove, I thought. "But whatever he used on top, whenever he painted it—the bottom layer would have to be old? If it didn't peel off?"

"If it is oil paint, then yes, at least one hundred years. Maybe two hundred."

"Maybe five hundred?"

Sanjiv laughed. "Yes, yes, my friend, maybe five hundred. Maybe one thousand. Maybe it is a painting from the cavemen."

"Okay, okay."

"You think it is valuable, yes? You should sell it, and then you would have enough money to buy toasty nuts."

I dug out a dollar (bringing me down to $320) and handed it to him. "Sanjiv, if this painting is what I think it is, I'll buy the whole cart."

"It's real! It's real!"

I attracted the attention of half of Katsanakis's Diner—except Bodhi. Her head was down, as usual, over her phone, the white line of her part stark between the two tight braids. "What's real?" she mumbled.

I rolled my eyes as I slid into the booth. "The painting, of course."

"What painting?"

My head spun. "What painting? Are you kidding me? The painting in my—"

Bodhi looked up with a grin, her face tan against her white button-down. "Gotcha. Did you really think I'd forget? C'mon, this is my new independent study project. I take that very seriously. And I got a lot of digging done on the retreat."

Oh. A joke. I settled back into the vinyl, relieved. "How was Morocco anyway?"

"Hot. How was New York?"

"Same."

A waitress stopped by and dropped two menus on the table. "What can I getcha?"

Bodhi looked at me. "Pie?"

"No, I just ate." I handed one of the menus back to the waitress. "Just ice water for me." The waitress frowned, but I didn't want to get into a habit of Bodhi paying for things. Or worse yet, to be expected to pick up the check next time.

"Okay," Bodhi shrugged. "One piece of cherry pie for me." She handed the menus back. "And water," she called after the woman's swishing backside before turning to me. "So what makes you say it's real?"

"Well, it's real old, that I know. See—"

"Did you look into hyperspectral imaging?" Bodhi cut me off.

"Well, no. It's just—"

"Or X-ray fluorescence mapping?" She was back tapping her phone again. "Or maybe dendrochronology, since it's painted on wood."

"Dendro-wha—no. What did *you* do—get a forensics degree? I thought you were camped out in some Moroccan monastery."

"I was. With Wi-Fi, remember? And since my mom spent most of her time whirling with the dervishes,

I enrolled myself at the University of Interwebs. Learned a lot about the dating techniques that are out there."

The waitress came back and placed a slice of pie, a generous slice of warm, flaky pie overstuffed with glistening cherries, in front of Bodhi.

I rattled my free ice cubes. "Well, I've been doing a lot of research, too. Listen to this." I laid out the whole conversation with Sanjiv, strengthening my grasp on the science as I reviewed it point by point. The more I talked, the more convinced I became.

Bodhi looked skeptical. "No offense to Sanjiv, but do you think Cadwalader's is going to accept expert testimony from the Toasty Nuts guy?"

"Who cares what they think? If the bottom layer of oil paint is as old as Sanjiv says it is, we know Jack didn't paint it himself. It's not a fake. Gemma was wrong. About that, at least."

"Welllll, maybe." Bodhi chewed thoughtfully, then stuffed another bite of pie in her mouth while I gnawed my ice cubes. "I would want to see an infrared reflectogram before I came to any conclusions. And what about the missing provenance? Did you find any reference to the painting, any list of former owners?"

The atmosphere in the booth shifted, and separated by the formica table, we suddenly felt more like rivals than teammates.

"What's going on?" I said, maybe a bit too defensively. "You're the one who said, 'Oh, this thing's worth thirty-seven million.'"

"That's before I did my research. Based on the evidence, I think it's pretty unlikely that you're going to suddenly find a Raphael or a Leonardo or even a Fra Angelico"—now she knew about Fra Angelico?— "just sitting around your house. I mean, these were big-time artists. They didn't just go around misplacing paintings."

"You sound like Gemma." Now I was the one spitting out her name.

"Well, that's a low blow," said Bodhi calmly. "I'm just telling you what my research is showing, and it's pointing—"

"Yes, and I'm telling you what *my* research is showing. And my research hasn't been spent on"—I hitched my chin at the phone cradled in her palm— "that thing. It's been spent *really* looking at *real* paintings by *real* painters in *real* museums. You've never even *seen* a Raphael. A real one, I mean,"

"And you have?"

"Sure, plenty of them. At the National Gallery. At the Frick. At the Met—"

"Okay, show me then." Bodhi's fork clattered to the table.

"Show you what?"

"A real Raphael. The Met's here in New York, right?" She threw some bills on the table, then scooted out of the booth, smearing a line of cherry juice across her white button-down. "Let's go check it out."

"What, right now?"

"Why not?" Bodhi looked down at me with a smirk. "Unless you've got something else on your agenda today?"

She knew I didn't. With one last look at the half-finished pie on the table, I slid out of the booth and followed Bodhi out the door.

Chapter Eight

Our debate-filled subway ride ($317.50) was interrupted by two separate mariachi bands, and an hour later we arrived at the Met. I wanted to head straight for the Italian Renaissance gallery, but Bodhi stood in the middle of the marbled main hall and declared that she wanted to see everything.

"Everything?" My head swiveled around to take in the North, South, and West entrances and wobbled briefly to imagine what lay behind them. "That would take weeks. Months even. I came here every single week, sometimes twice or even three times a week, with my grandfather, and even *I* haven't seen everything."

"Well then, we'd better get going."

I led Bodhi to the admissions desk, where I handed over my usual penny ($317.49) and Bodhi put the full, recommended amount on her Plati-

num Card. We affixed the green metal "M" buttons
to our collars and headed straight for the perennial
tourist favorite, the Temple of Dendur.

Bodhi was fascinated by the temple. She insisted
on viewing it from every angle, she snapped photos
of the hieroglyphics and tried to decode them via an
app she downloaded then and there. She was particularly taken with the eighteenth-century graffiti.
"OnDa1 would not believe this!" she said as she took
another photo and sent it off to her rapper friend.
"We did a whole unit on graffiti trends as part of my
history of hip-hop study."

When she finally grew tired of the temple, she wandered over to the wishing pool and flipped in a coin.

"Guess what I wished for?"

"I don't know, what?"

"Nah, I can't tell you or it won't come true." She
arranged her braids behind her ears. "Okay, what's
next?"

It seemed that the research Bodhi had performed over her vacation had not only made her
a self-styled expert on art authentication, but had
also sparked a love of art in general.

Bodhi's enthusiasm was infectious, and I found
myself racing to show her all my favorite spots in
the museum. The room-sized optical illusion of the

Gubbio Studiolo. The Chinese garden. The giant Buddha and his outsized sense of peace. The psychedelic "figure five in gold." The Islamic prayer niche, like a stained-glass window in tiles, festooned with actual prayers. The two self-portraits of French women painters, canvases hung side by side, shown at their craft in the dead middle of a museum full of craftsmen. Crafts*men*.

Bodhi developed her own way to experience the museum. For example, taking on the pose of a Greek statue and waiting for a tourist to bump into you. Or loudly browsing the galleries like a rich housewife. ("How much for the Warhol? Nah, I'll wait for the sales.") She invented an elaborate scavenger hunt that involved finding items in paintings whose first letters spelled out a secret message. And came up with a game called Attack!, which involved nothing more than hiding behind the suits of armor and jumping out to yell "Attack!" at each other.

"Hey, girls, knock it off! This is a museum, not a playground."

I recognized the Trinidadian accent and turned around to see Bernadette, one of the guards who'd worked with my grandfather.

"Theo, is that you? Come over here and give me some sugar, girl."

Bernadette wrapped me in a warm embrace, her buttons cold against my cheek, like Jack's.

"If I'd known it was you, I wouldn't have talked so rough. But you got to keep it quiet. The muckety-mucks are punchy these days."

"How come?"

"I'll tell you how come." Bernadette looked around and then leaned in. "A painting's been stolen."

Bodhi and I froze.

"Really?" I whispered. "When did that happen?"

Bernadette savored the piece of news in her mouth like a slowly melting chocolate. "About a month ago. Maybe even longer. They don't really know, you see. The painting had been sent down to storage a while back, but when they went to collect it for some exhibition—poof!—it was gone."

"Poof, huh? Just like that?" Bodhi looked at me.

"Just like that. So now they don't want no funny business in the galleries. You girls keep it down, you hear me? And Theo, baby girl, don't you be a stranger. I miss your grandpa. He was a tough old nut, but he was a good nut, still."

Bernadette's news had a sobering effect on us, and without exchanging a word, Bodhi and I both directed our feet to the task at hand.

In the Met's Italian Renaissance rooms, we passed Ghirlandaios and Mantegnas and Botticellis and soon found ourselves in front of the Met's only resident Raphael, the *Colonna Altarpiece*

We stood there for quite a while, frozen in a hushed awe.

"Wow," Bodhi finally murmured.

"Yeah," I responded.

"It's so . . ."

"Yeah, so . . ."

"So . . ."

"So . . ."

"Eh," Bodhi finally pronounced.

"Yeah," I sighed. "Eh."

"I mean, it's—"

"Beautiful," I nodded.

"And—"

"Refined."

"And—"

"Ethereal."

"I was going to say boring," said Bodhi. "But I can see ethereal."

"It's just that *our* painting," by now it was known as ours, "is so—"

"Deep," mused Bodhi.

"And—"

"Sad."

"And—"

"Real."

"I was going to say complexly nuanced," I said, retrieving a phrase from some book somewhere. "But real is right."

We fell into silence again.

"I know you don't want to hear this," Bodhi finally ventured gently. "But I know you see it, too. The painting in your attic does not look like this one."

I readjusted the strap of my sweater bag, which was digging into my shoulder. "I know. But—"

"But nothing." Bodhi pointed at the altarpiece, with its serene Madonna and bouncing baby Jesus and John the Baptist, and its grave and pious saints. "This is, you know, so still and . . . well, flawless. Ours has . . . edge?"

"Soul," I corrected her.

"Yeah, soul," Bodhi nodded.

Bodhi was right.

But I knew I was, too.

"You know, this altarpiece is a perfect example of something that's been bothering me." I plunked myself in the middle of the floor and laid out the books from my bag. "Stylistically, our painting is a match. The brushwork, the coloring—the technical aspects, Jack would call them, the ways that the painter actually designed the painting and applied the paint. They look just like this altarpiece." I flipped around the books until I found reproductions of Raphael's famous Madonna and Child compositions, side by side. "But in tone, it's no match at all. See these Madonnas? Just like the altarpiece, right? They're perfect. They're perfectly loving, perfectly peaceful—"

"Perfectly boring," said Bodhi, who was now crouching next to me.

"Well, you could say that. They're idealized, is what they are. They aren't meant to look like real people. They're meant to be—what's the word?—inaccessible. They're supposed to be otherworldy—literally from another world."

"You mean heaven?"

"Exactly." I grabbed another book out of my bag. "Now look at this one. This painting is by Raphael, too. It's a noblewoman named," I checked the bottom of the page, "Elisabetta Gonzaga."

The face looking out from the book seemed to regard us with disdain, her lids lowered, not even a hint of a smile on her lips.

Bodhi whistled. "She looks like a real—"

"I know. Doesn't she look like someone you would actually meet?"

"She looks like someone I would avoid."

"Right! You get a sense of her whole personality, warts and all. Or look at this one."

I found an ancient, bearded man, cloaked in red.

"That's one craggy dude," offered Bodhi.

"That's Pope Julius II, Raphael's most important patron. He died shortly after the portrait was painted."

"Are you sure he didn't die *while* the portrait was painted?"

"He looks exhausted, right? Beaten down. Not what you'd expect in a portrait of the most powerful man in the world.

"Or look at this one." I showed Bodhi a fat man whose wandering eye was only somewhat masked by the way he gazed up at heaven. "Raphael didn't 'fix' any of these people's flaws. He presented them as they were. Not perfect, just human."

"Well, it's no wonder they all look like real people."

"What do you mean?"

"Jeesh, who's the art expert now?" Bodhi cocked her head and looked at me. "They *are* real people. All of these paintings you just showed me are portraits."

Of course. They weren't models, airbrushed into

saints and angels. They were real people. These were portraits.

So did that mean that our painting was also—

"Why, can this be the fair Theodora Tenpenny squatting in our midst?"

Bodhi and I looked up to find a tall but stooped elderly man in a starched linen suit leaning over us, his hands clasped around a silver-topped cane.

"Mr. Randolph!" I pulled Bodhi to her feet and made her stick out her hand. "Hi! I was just showing my friend Bodhi here the wing."

"How do you do, Miss Brody?" The man shook her hand importantly, but before Bodhi could correct him, he turned to me with his arms out. "Now, Theodora, who is this 'Mr. Randolph'? How many times do I have to tell you to call me Uncle Lydon?"

I submitted to a limp-armed hug, my face crushing the fresh pink carnation in his lapel. As the head curator for the European Paintings collection, Lydon Randolph had been Jack's boss at the museum. But for some reason, Lydon preferred to think of himself as an important patron of Jack's career, providing the day job that allowed him to keep painting.

As I retreated from the hug, Lydon caught my hand in his. "My sweet Theodora," he purred in the nurtured accent of the displaced Southern aristocrat, "how sorry I was to hear of your grandfather's passing."

I thought back to that stain on Spinney Street, and the term, "passing," didn't seem to capture it.

"He was as much a fixture of this wing as a Rembrandt. As were you, come to think of it." He dropped my hand and gestured at the marble floor. "I can't tell you the number of times I found you in just that position, hunched over your crayons. But no more crayons, I see," he said, his eye landing on one of the books at my feet. He leaned over with effort, plucking up the volume while using his cane for balance. *"The People and Portraits of Raffaello Sanzio,* eh? An excellent resource, though better in the original Italian." He handed the book back to me. "A bit of light summer reading?"

I stuffed the book in my bag and quickly gathered up the rest of the books scattered on the floor. "Well, like I said, I was just showing my friend Bodhi here around." I turned to Bodhi and raised my eyebrows in warning. "Mr. Randolph—I mean, um, Uncle Lydon—is the head curator for the European Paintings wing," I said emphatically.

"Emeritus," Lydon proffered with a gracious bow.

"What does that mean?" Bodhi picked at a mosquito bite.

"In layman's terms, my dear," Lydon tried the same bow again, "retired."

"So why are you here?"

Lydon coughed up the faint laugh that adults use when they actually find you annoying. "Yes, well, one of many perks of five decades' employment at the Metropolitan Museum is an office onsite for ongoing research and mentorship."

Bodhi's face lit up, and I knew immediately that no good could come from whatever she was going to say.

"Fifty years? That's a long time. You must know everything about this place."

He chuckled. "Well, I'm not sure that my oversight would extend to—"

"Like, you would know if a painting had gone missing or something."

I raised my eyebrows at Bodhi and again attempted to telegraph S-H-U-T U-P.

Lydon drew up his lean frame a bit. "The Metropolitan Museum has not had a painting stolen since its opening in 1872. Now the Gardner Museum in Boston, there's a fascinating tale—"

"That's not what I heard."

Lydon looked silently at Bodhi, then even longer at me. "I beg your pardon?"

"I heard"—Bodhi shot me what she must have thought was a secret wink—"*we* heard that you're missing a painting. Any ideas what happened to it?"

With a glance around the room, Lydon snapped, "Come with me, girls," and turned on the heel of his freshly polished shoe, striding briskly—more briskly than you would expect of a man with a cane—out of the gallery.

"What are you doing?" I hissed to Bodhi as I trotted behind him, just out of earshot.

"We can tease out how much he knows!" Bodhi hissed back.

"It doesn't matter what he knows. Now he's going to know how much we know!"

"Whoops, didn't think about that." She shrugged. "Sorry."

We followed Lydon through galleries, elevators, semi-hidden doorways, and institutional-looking corridors, until we arrived at a book-lined office with a sweeping view of Central Park and Lydon's name in brass on the door.

Lydon gestured for us to sit in two straight-backed chairs and took his place behind an imposing mahogany desk.

"Now, girls," he produced a fountain pen and

rested it under his chin with a composed smile, "what's all this about?"

I put my hand firmly on Bodhi's arm before she could speak. "Nothing. We just overheard some guards talking about a missing painting. That's all."

Lydon shifted uncomfortably in his chair. "Well, then, you know better than to believe rumors."

"Sure, yes, just a rumor," I agreed quickly.

"People—employees especially—like to gossip. Turn a minor misunderstanding into something notable, something salacious."

"Um, sure. I guess."

"Your grandfather was a valued employee of the Met for many, many years. I'm sure he would be *deeply* disappointed to think you were spreading stories—fictions really—that besmirch the reputation of this museum. *And* its security team." He looked at me pointedly over the top of his spectacles.

I looked pointedly back. "Jack didn't care about reputations—his own *or* the museum's. The only thing he cared about was the art."

"Why, yes, Theodora. You're right. He did care deeply about the museum's collection. And wouldn't he prioritize the safety of that art above all else?"

I thought back to the painting in his studio, painted

over and hidden for decades. Hidden for its safe-keeping, I suddenly saw. "Yes," I nodded slowly. "Yes, he would."

Lydon stood up and came around to the front of his desk, looming over us like an eclipse. "And that's why we mustn't go around repeating these stories—which have no basis in fact, I should add—which can only confuse people." He settled himself on the desk's corner. "And we don't want to confuse people, do we?"

"What are you guys talking about?" Bodhi piped up. "The truth is, you're missing a painting. How is telling people the truth about it confusing them?"

Lydon's concerned-uncle façade faltered. "Look, girls, I don't want word getting out about any of this—period. This is a small but significant paint-ing of great value. If word gets out, we could lose it to the underground art market forever, especially if people believe it's in unsecured hands."

"Oh, it's not unsecured," Bodhi blurted out, then looked at me and slapped her hand over her mouth.

The small room filled with a menacing silence.

"It's not possible. There's no way that painting could have left this building. Not past our security—" Lydon stopped himself.

I said nothing, as did (thank God) Bodhi.

Lydon began agitatedly tapping his fountain pen on his knee.

"It's no secret that Jack always had financial issues," he mused aloud, "despite the work I secured for him over the years." Blue ink began to spatter Lydon's crisp trousers with each tap of his pen. "But perhaps Jack had a 'retirement plan' in place, hmmm? One that involved removing the painting and leaving it, for some reason, in the hands of a ten-year-old girl—"

"Thirteen," I corrected.

Lydon leaped to his feet and grabbed my arm, oblivious to the inky fingerprints he left.

"Listen, you little brat. You think you can walk into a pawnshop with a de Kooning under your arm? They'll arrest you so fast—"

"De Kooning?" I gasped. "What are you talking about?"

"Yes, of course the de Kooning. The missing painting." Lydon cleared his throat. "I mean, the painting rumored to be missing."

Even I knew that Willem de Kooning was a twentieth-century Dutch abstract painter. Who most definitely did not go around painting the Virgin Mary.

Lydon was talking about a different painting.

But before I could do damage control—

"Who's de Kooning?" piped up Bodhi. "I thought we were talking about Raphael."

Lydon stared at Bodhi and slowly released his grip on my arm.

"What are you talking about?"

"Nothing." I glared at Bodhi who finally clamped her lips shut.

Lydon sat back and regarded me. "My God, there's another painting, isn't there?" he put together slowly. He looked at my sweater bag, bulging with its tomes on the Italian Renaissance. "A Raphael," he whispered.

Bodhi jumped up and pulled the arm recently vacated by Lydon's grip toward the door. "Nope. There's no missing painting, remember? That's what you said. So I guess this conversation never happened."

We were almost to the stairs by the time Lydon made it to the door. I don't know what made him madder—our escape or his ink-stained suit—but the last thing we heard in the stairwell was the bouncing echo of a four-letter word.

Chapter Nine

We didn't stop running until we were halfway through Central Park, finally giving in at the roller skaters' circle. It took most of "Disco Inferno" before we'd caught our breath enough to talk.

"So," Bodhi wheezed, "that guy was talking about some other painting. A de Korn— de Koon—"

"A de Kooning. Yeah," I nodded wearily.

"So Jack stole that one, too?"

I paused to massage a stitch in my side. "I don't think he stole either of them," I started slowly. "I mean, there is still a chance that Jack smuggled our painting out—what, forty years ago? But honestly, if they're this keyed up about a minor de Kooning gone missing in the last year or so, they'd have conducted a full-scale manhunt already for a missing Raphael."

"So we still don't know where he got it?"

"No." I sighed heavily. "But Lydon had a good point. I can't walk into a pawnshop with this thing, or an antiques shop, or—"

"Cadwalader's? They didn't even think it was real."

"That's because Gemma is an idiot. Nice shoes and all, but still an idiot."

"No argument here." Bodhi flopped herself under a tree.

"Okay, maybe it's stolen," I said as I collapsed next to her, too hot to care about the dirt being ground into my petticoat. "But maybe it isn't. Maybe he got it honestly. All I know is, if I can't figure out where he got it and find some kind of proof of ownership, then they're going to assume it's stolen. And it's going to be taken away before I can figure out why Jack wanted me to have it in the first place."

"And before you can sell it."

"That, too."

We eventually left the cool shade of the park and made our way slowly down Broadway (picking up a decent-looking castoff blender along the way). By the time we reached Spinney Lane, the sun was slipping beyond New Jersey.

Bodhi paused in front of our house, hitching a foot up on our stoop. "So do you think it's a portrait?"

The same question had been rattling around my brain all the way down Broadway. "I don't know. Raphael used La Fornarina as a model for the Virgin Mary plenty of times before. But every other time, he'd transformed her into this perfectly idealized Madonna. Why not this time?"

"Because this time—"

"This time he was painting the real Margherita Luti, his one true love. And if that's the case, then—"

"Who's the kid?"

"Exactly."

Bodhi nodded distractedly and walked off toward her own house without even a good-bye. But as I got the key in the front door, I heard sneakers pounding on the sidewalk, and Bodhi appeared again under the light of the streetlamp. "Here's another question," she panted. "That bird is flying out of the baby's hand, right? I saw a bunch of paintings at the Met today with Jesus and birds, but those birds were all flying down. All white and golden and shiny with light."

"Wow," I said, "you really were paying attention."

"Hey, I told you, this is my new independent study project." She grinned. "And I'm gonna get an A."

Bodhi vowed to barricade herself in her media room and not to leave her computer until she uncovered proof that determined the painting's authenticity, or history, or both.

I retired to the kitchen, my books splayed all over the table, which is where I was when my mom wandered in around midnight and started opening cupboard doors at random.

"Mom? What are you doing out—I mean, up?" It was rare to see my mom outside her room beyond her morning walk to the tea shop.

"Oh, Theo, there you are. I was calling for you. I'm out of tea." She started rummaging under the sink, among the buckets and cleaners. "The kettle?"

Sigh. "I got it." I snagged the kettle from its usual place on the stove and filled it at the sink. "What's up? You stuck on something?"

My mom sank into one of the unmatched kitchen chairs and stared out the darkened window. "An equation. I can't sleep."

"Me too."

Her eyes, puffy under heavy lids, fluttered down to the books on the table. "Oh, really? Is it some kind of Diophantine equation? Because I could help—"

"Well, not an equation exactly. A problem."

"Maybe I could take a look," she murmured as she opened the big monograph.

"I dunno. It's not math." I put Mrs. Tenpenny III's chipped china tea service on the table and threw in a (clean) old nylon stocking stuffed with loose chamomile leaves. "It's something for Jack."

"Oh." I heard my mom start humming as she flipped absently through the pages. She didn't like thinking about his death, and I could tell her brain had taken refuge in a theorem again.

I put a flowery teacup and saucer in front of her. "Careful with that book, please. It's not mine."

"I *am* being careful," she said. Like a child. Then she peeked in the pitcher. "Is there any milk?"

"No," I responded testily. Not for a month.

"Oh, dear." My mom drifted back to the monograph. "You'd better get some at the deli tomorrow."

The teakettle whistled, and my mother made no move for it, engrossed in the monograph, her fingers lightly skimming the chubby cheeks of a Raphael baby.

"Oh, now, don't you move. Let me get that for you," I said. Maybe a bit too loudly.

"These pictures," she said, "they're just so—" She left the thought there and slowly turned the pages, in hopes the word she was searching for would appear on the next page.

I poured the steaming water into the teapot. "Yes, they're Raphaels. I've just rediscovered them, too. Jack always liked them, didn't he? They are very—"

"Symmetrical."

Symmetrical? I looked over my mom's shoulder to see which painting she was talking about. All of them, it seemed, as she kept flipping pages.

"You're talking about the Madonna and Child paintings, right? I mean, there's a sense of balance and harmony between the figures, but it's not exactly mirror symmetry—"

"But there's such perfection," she said as she traced a page with her finger. "The mother and the child, like two equal sides of an equation."

In our case, that would be an imbalanced equation, I thought. "They're just mothers and babies, Mom."

"No, the perfect mothers. The perfect love. Look, see?"

I leaned over, planting my hands on the table, to see the *Madonna della Seggiola,* one of Raphael's best-known Madonna-Child compositions. Mom had a point. The mother here—her little dumpling snuggled under her cheek—resembled a happier, more peaceful version of the Virgin Mary in the painting upstairs. For a moment, a sense of calm settled over the dank kitchen.

Then Mom flipped to the very beginning of the book, pushing it toward me. "And this one, too."

La Fornarina graced the title page, in that topless girlie-mag pose.

I snickered. "Uh well, that's hardly the Virgin Mary, Mom. It's Raphael's mistress."

Mom smiled a wistful smile. "No, she's a mother. See the way she's touching her breast? I did that when you were a baby, too. To remember which side I'd last fed you on. When you were hungry, I'd check to see which side felt full."

Ew.

"I took care of you once," she murmured, and she absently reached out to place her hand on mine.

Now you have to understand—my mother had "a need for solitude," my grandfather called it. She was "not a hugger," he sometimes said. "Touch aversion" was a term I came across in a psychology manual once. Whatever the name or the reason, I was surprised— no, shocked—to feel her hand closing over mine.

So maybe I can be forgiven for instinctively snatching my hand away.

But would Eddie forgive me for spilling an entire pot of tea on the For Reference Only monograph?

"Towels! We need towels, Mom!" I screeched. I ransacked the kitchen and grabbed whatever threadbare dish towels I could find, throwing them on the table to stave off the chamomile flood.

I looked up from my frantic dabbing and swiping to see my mom holding the empty teapot out to me. "Is there any more water?" She dangled the sagging stocking in the air. "I saved the tea."

I took a deep breath. Then I retrieved the kettle and refilled her teapot, which she held gingerly by the handle and spout and took back upstairs to her nest.

It must be nice, I thought as I began to individually blot pages 10 through 107, to always be the chubby, helpless baby in the family. Or better yet, a flittering, nervous bird perched so precariously that everyone tiptoes around, trying not to scare it away.

And what if I did scare her away? What difference would it make, except to save me tea shop bills we couldn't pay anyway?

But I knew. It would mean that the Tenpennys weren't the Tenpennys anymore. It would just be the name on the door of a house I used to live in. Before I went to foster care.

And then I would be really, truly, entirely alone.

It took me another hour to blot and dry each page of the monograph individually, and I was finally heading upstairs for a cold bath when I heard banging at the door.

There was only one reason for banging on the door in the middle of the night. The jig is up, I thought as I fumbled for a reasonable explanation of why I'd let weeks go by without turning in a stolen painting to the cops. But when I wrenched open the front door, I found Bodhi dancing around in the stoop's shadows.

"Where's the painting? Where is it?" she said breathlessly.

I waved Bodhi inside. "Upstairs, of course. Why?" I stepped out on the stoop and looked around. No idling police cars.

"Well, go get it! And bring that big book on Raphael, too. We're going on a field trip!"

"Now? Can't it wait till tomorrow?"

"No way. We'll have better luck tonight."

"With what?" As I stepped back inside, I saw by the meager hall light that Bodhi's right arm hung strangely at her side.

"With my broken arm."

Chapter Ten

No matter how urgent your medical emergency or dire your prospects, the ER staff always made sure you spent plenty of time in the waiting room. But for us it was time needed for Bodhi to explain her latest theory. And her unhinged arm.

I found us some unoccupied plastic molded chairs in one corner, which was lucky because some drunks had claimed the other rows as beds. "Okay," Bodhi sat down, arranging her right arm on her lap and checking her phone one-handed, "what do you know about La Fornarina?"

I placed the Samsonite heavily on the floor. "Wait a minute. What happened to your arm?"

"Sit down. I'll get to it. But what do you know about La Fornarina?"

"What do *you* know about La Fornarina?"

"Well, tonight after dinner I was Googling Raphael-plus-all the different conservation technologies, to see if anyone had found any clues that way—you know, through infrared or whatever. And I found this one article." Bodhi was swiping and poking furiously with one hand at her phone's screen.

"Okay, check this out. Do you know this painting?" The phone in my face showed the same topless painting I'd just flooded with tea.

"Sure, that's Raphael's famous portrait of La Fornarina."

"Right. So a few years back they were restoring it, and they X-rayed it for some reason—"

"Probably to see if there are original sketches underneath. Or changes that were painted out. Jack said artists sometimes make changes along the way, so the X-ray can reveal what their original intent was."

"Well, check out this original intent. They X-rayed La Fornarina and found this." Bodhi zoomed in on the image and held it up for me to see.

There, on Margherita Luti's ring finger, on the left hand that lay demurely on her lap, was the outline of a ring.

"It's a ring with a square red ruby. Painted over, probably by Raphael's student," Bodhi checked the article again, "Giulio Romano, who sold the painting after Raphael died."

I blinked. "It's on her wedding finger."

"Exactly!" Bodhi bounced in her chair.

"But they weren't married. He was engaged to someone else—"

"—who he strung along for seven years, remember?" Bodhi had read the article and everything. "Now we know why."

"So Raphael had to hide his marriage to La Fornarina because . . ."

"No," Bodhi huffed impatiently, "you aren't paying attention. Raphael painted the ring in. He *wanted* it there. After Raphael died, his *student* is the one who painted it out. Right before he sold it."

"Because—"

"Because what would a painting by the recently deceased superstar of the art world sell for if it showed he was married to the daughter of a baker?"

I didn't know what surprised me more: the revelation of the ruby ring, or Bodhi's transformation into a Raphael expert. Or how irritated I was that she'd made such a brilliant discovery.

"So you got me out of bed—"

"You weren't in bed."

"I was going to bed," I pouted. "You dragged me

out of bed, got out my," I lowered my voice, "*suitcase,* made me sit here in this creepy waiting room in the middle of the night—just to show me that article?"

"No, stupid." Bodhi pointed to her arm. "How else are we going to X-ray our painting?"

The ER night shift was skeptical of Bodhi's arm injury, and at least wanted to wait for her parents to show up before green-lighting any expensive medical procedures. But after Bodhi squeezed out two fat tears and whispered, "I don't want them to hurt me again," the head doc went ahead and sent her for X-rays, with me for moral support, while they scrambled to find a social worker.

I had to admit, Bodhi had a certain talent—and not just for popping her arm out of its socket at will.

"Okay, so what do we do next?" I whispered as Bodhi was wheeled toward the X-ray room.

"Shut up, I didn't think we'd get this far," Bodhi said between clenched teeth.

"You didn't think we'd *what?*"

I switched the suitcase to my other sweaty hand and fumed all over again. Having a partner in crime is nice and all. Except when they add medical insurance fraud to your list of crimes.

But as they wheeled her into the X-ray lab, I saw

Bodhi relax and smile. I followed her eyes to a copy of the *New York Post*, opened to Page Six, on the technician's console. She composed her face back into that of a helpless waif and turned around to the orderly.

"I'm scared. Is that social worker here yet?" She blinked rapidly and summoned a fresh tear to trail down her cheek.

"Lemme go check, hon. You'll be okay with Larry here."

As soon as the door closed behind the orderly, Bodhi jumped out of the wheelchair and yelped as she popped her arm back into the socket, much to Larry the X-ray technician's surprise.

"Okay, Larry, here's the deal. My arm is fine. We need you to X-ray something else."

Larry, a pasty man who'd apparently spent too much of his life in dark rooms, stopped his Krispy Kreme in midbite. Bodhi kicked my leg and gestured to open the suitcase.

"It's this painting. If we do this fast, you won't get in trouble. Just one good image is all we need." By now, I had the painting out, and Bodhi was directing me to position it against the wall. "Okay, let's go. That orderly will be back any minute."

Seeing a painting where he usually saw body parts

finally roused the technician. "Hold on, what's going on here?" He put down the doughnut and reached for the phone. "I'm calling Dr. Chen."

Bodhi left the painting and sprung across the room to the technician's station. "Wait a minute, do you know Jake Ford? The actor?"

Larry's interest was piqued. "Yeah, of course. So what?"

"What about Jessica Blake?"

A twinkle of excitement appeared in the man's dull eyes. "Jessica Blake? Sure!"

"Would you like her autograph?" Bodhi rummaged in a tote bag I hadn't noticed before and pulled out a glossy head shot, which she dangled over the buttons and knobs of the man's desk. Then she whisked it away. "Or maybe you'd like something . . . more valuable?"

The technician's eyes stayed fixed on the head shot. "Like what?"

Bodhi turned the head shot over and grabbed a Sharpie off the desk. "This is the number of the editor of Page Six," she muttered with the Sharpie cap between her teeth, jotting a series of numbers on the back of the photo. "You call her in the morning—she won't get in before ten—and you tell her that Jessica Blake will be at this address," more jotting, "at this time tomorrow. Trust me, she'll be very grateful for the information. *Very.*"

Larry nodded slowly. "Okay. Okay, yeah, that sounds . . . doable." His sticky hand reached for the head shot, but not before Bodhi could yank it off the table again.

"First, let's take some pictures."

I'd never had the misfortune of needing an X-ray, but in my head, I thought they used some big machine and an hour later you got some film that the doctor held up to a lightbulb to read.

But it seems that X-rays have gone the way of Bodhi's phone, with computerized functions, on-screen zooms, digital enhancements. Luckily Larry was as good at his job as he was at putting down doughnuts. He zoomed in on La Fornarina's ring finger, and by adjusting the contrast, color spectrum, and a bunch of other things I didn't understand, was able to find what had been hidden for five hundred years.

There on his computer screen, sketched lightly in white against the dark gray of the third finger, was a ring with a square-cut stone.

"It's there! It's there!" Bodhi hugged me with her left arm and started jumping up and down. "I knew it! It's a Raphael for sure. I told you it was!"

"You never—"

"Oh, shut up. It's a Raphael, okay? You're rich!"

Larry looked up. "You're what?"

I started jumping along with Bodhi. "We did it!"

"Do you guys need these files?" Larry started dragging files around on-screen.

"Yeah, burn us a CD. And we need hard copies, too!" Bodhi turned to me. "Eat our X-rays, Gemma! Am I right?"

"Bodhi, that orderly is going to be back any second. We'd better get packed up." I moved to grab the painting, but Bodhi stopped me.

"Wait a second. Larry, let's get one more shot of the whole picture." She looked at me. "Hey, maybe there's some more original intent under there."

Larry zoomed out, made a little more dashboard magic, and brought the entire canvas in view on his screen.

It was strange to see the painting, with its intricate coloring, reduced to a grayed-out skeleton sketch of images.

But it was even stranger to see a ghostly apparition lurking behind the Madonna and Child.

The city was just coming to life by the time we made it out of the hospital, the official X-ray films hidden in the Samsonite along with the painting and the CD in Bodhi's back pocket.

"How's your arm?" I asked Bodhi as we grabbed a window seat at the diner. ("Breakfast is on me," said Bodhi. "Eggs?" I shook my head. "Pancakes.")

"S'okay." Bodhi rubbed her right shoulder. "It hurts when I pop it in and out like that. But it was worth it."

We laid out the X-ray films on the Formica, careful not to splash our bottomless cups of coffee.

"So it's a person?" Bodhi yawned.

I held the film up to the window for a better look. "A man. It must have been painted out, too. Maybe at the same time as the ring."

"That's weird."

I thought for a second. "Not necessarily. Raphael painted some Holy Family paintings—you know, Mary, Joseph, and Jesus together. Maybe that student, Romano, who painted out the ring—maybe he thought it would be worth more with just Mary and Jesus."

I hauled out the trusty monograph again and found a few examples of Holy Family paintings clustered together toward the back of the book. "See, it's a pretty common composition. There's Mary sitting with Jesus. And then Joseph is usually standing behind them, kind of looking over them, like our painted-out man is. Joseph usually has this staff or cane or big stick of some kind."

Bodhi snatched up the X-ray. "I can't tell a lot from this, but there's definitely no stick." I took it back and looked, too. It was true. The man behind the Madonna and Child held nothing, resting one arm on the Virgin's shoulder and the other reaching toward the Christ Child.

"There's something else weird," I ventured. "No beard."

"What are you talking about?" Bodhi tapped at the man's outline. "There's a beard right there." She was right. The man sported the outline of a mustache and closely cropped beard, which matched the dark hair that he wore in a pageboy parted down the middle.

"But not the right kind. Joseph is supposed to have a long, gray beard and a bald head. It's part of his iconography."

"What's that?"

"You doofus, didn't you hear anything Reverend Cecily said?" It thrilled me a little to have a friend I could insult so casually. "Iconography. Like, every saint or figure has things that identify them. So John the Baptist is always wearing animal skins, because he wandered the wilderness. And Saint Peter always has keys, because he holds the keys to heaven. And the Virgin Mary is always wearing blue, because it was the most expensive color in the artist's paint box. They made the paint out of crushed jewels."

Bodhi took a slurp of her coffee.

"Well, our Virgin isn't wearing blue. She's wearing gray. Gray and white."

Bodhi was right. A drab gray dress with white sleeves.

"And another thing," Bodhi peeked at the monograph again, "these guys in the book are wearing—what are those? Togas?"

"Yes, togas. It was part of the whole Renaissance obsession with classical Greek and—"

Bodhi tapped the X-ray and the window behind it again. "Well, there's no toga here. No toga, no long beard, no stick."

There was something familiar about the specter behind the Madonna and Child. The way he gazed directly at the viewer with his large, round eyes. The familiarity of the hand on the Virgin's shoulder. The hair and the beard and the—

"Oh. My. God."

I dropped the film and paged frantically through the monograph, stopping at a painting of two men.

"What's that one called?" Bodhi asked.

"It's a painting called *Self-Portrait with a Friend.*" I propped up the book for Bodhi to see. "Look at the man standing in back."

"Self-portrait?" Bodhi's eyes widened. "That's . . . ?"

"Yes," I nodded. "That's Raphael himself. And so," I held up the X-ray again, "is that."

Chapter Eleven

It wasn't a Madonna and Child. Or even a Holy Family. It was a family portrait.

A family portrait of Raffaello Sanzio, his secret wife, and his sleeping child. Making this the only painting—the only record of any kind—that proved the existence of Raphael's family.

Suddenly everything made sense.

It explained why the woman and child looked so human, so complex, and nothing like gods.

It explained why Margherita Luti—not the Virgin Mary—was identified with the pearl (*margarita*) in her hair.

It explained the hand on the boob. For once my mother was right: Raphael was trying to tell us—across three different paintings—that she was not just a mistress, but a mother.

But I still didn't understand what had transformed the sexy and sensuous Fornarina into such a melancholy figure.

And I was haunted by an even bigger question: What happened to the child? Vasari never mentions him—or her, for that matter—and he tells us that, on his deathbed, Raphael sent his mistress away, "leaving her the means to live a good and decent life." According to the monograph, records show that Margherita Luti entered a convent four months after his death—alone.

So was the child left in an orphanage? Made the charge of a powerful cardinal's household? Was he or she given a new name and some money and stashed with a bankrupt aristocrat?

Even three cups of Mr. Katsanakis's coffee couldn't revive us enough to tackle these questions, so Bodhi and I parted ways, me heading home to tend the chickens, the garden, and the teapot, and Bodhi to make sure her mother was photographed at 4:00, leaving the Kabbalah Centre instead of her plastic surgeon's office.

A thud at the front door woke me sometime in the hot, drowsy afternoon. I stumbled downstairs expecting another revelation by Bodhi, but found only a hand-written note from Madame Dumont ("I have not forgotten this rude business with the eggs. Nevertheless, I consider legalle action with my council . . .") and a thick manila envelope slid through the mail slot.

Return address: National Military Personnel Records Center.

I tore open the envelope right there in the hallway, pulling out a sheaf of papers and a cover letter introducing the military record I had requested for "Private First Class John Thornton Tenpenny V."

Some of the pages were stamped "CLASSIFIED" and then "DECLASSIFIED" with a date. Some had lines or words blacked out with marker. Most were filled with sections like this:

Hq. 1704th SU, Ft. Hamilton Ny From 21 SEP 1943 to 30 NOV 1943

Assd 69ID 423IR CQM 1 DEC 1943

632 135, CTST, Httsburg Miss. From 2 DEC 1943 to 11 JUL 1944

Tfr 28ID 321IR BQM 12 JUL 1944

POE Boston Ma, USS Yarmouth From 18 JUL 1944 to 23 JUL 1944

South. Cmmn, Eng., C18 From 23 JUL 1944 to 18 AUG 1944

I had a better chance of decoding Latin on my own. Once again, I was going to need a translator.

"Sweet! You got it!"

Eddie did a celebratory 360 in his desk chair. "You juiced my interest, you know, and I started looking into military records. Do you know how lucky you are? There was a fire in their archives in 1973, and the government lost most of its World War II–era files. I thought your granddad's file was a goner for sure." He grabbed the papers out of my hands and held them aloft over his head. "But it's alive! It's aliiiive!" A few patrons shot annoyed looks at Eddie. "Sorry, dudes, this is big," he announced.

I watched him thumb through until he reached some kind of career summary.

"Okay, here's the name, rank, serial number. . . . Now look here. As we already know, he enlisted right after Pearl Harbor. He joined up with the New York 69th Infantry. They did their training in Mississippi—"

"Mississippi?" I tried to imagine Jack, who dreaded even leaving the island of Manhattan, traveling south of the Mason-Dixon Line.

"Yup, Hattiesburg, it says. Then he got transferred to the 28th Infantry and was shipped over to England before finally hitting the European theater in August of 1944; looks like they acted as replacements for some of the boys who went in on D-Day. Went through Northern France—wow!—saw the liberation of Paris, then headed into Belgium. And look here—he was captured!"

"Captured? By who?"

"By who? By the Germans, that's who! See, it says he was sent to Stalag IX-B."

"Where's that?"

"Well, 'stalag' means camp or prison. This must have been a POW camp." Eddie took in my blank expression. "Prisoner-of-war, that is."

POW? It was one of those terms I'd heard somewhere before, but couldn't exactly picture it. And honestly, I wasn't sure I wanted to.

"What's this part that says 'classified'?"

Eddie studied the paper again. "Hmmmm, 'Classified January through March 1945." He looked up. "I don't know. There are a lot of reasons why the information might be classified. He could have been on a secret mission—"

"Like a spy?"

"Maybe. Maybe just pulled the short straw for some classified maneuver. Wherever he was, he turns up again in a French military hospital in

April of 1945. Doesn't say what he was treated for, just that he was released into a different division a couple of weeks later—let's see, the Civil Affairs division as part of the Monuments, Fine Arts, and Archives program? Wait a minute, is that—" Eddie entered the term into his computer. "No way!"

"What is it?"

"Your granddad wasn't just a soldier. He was one of the Monuments Men!"

"The what?"

"Hold on. This is indisputably rad. Like, historically rad." He seated me at a nearby table and came back ten minutes later with a stack of books from the history section.

He opened one of the books to a glossy middle section filled with black-and-white photographs. "These were the Monuments Men. A bunch of artists, curators, architects, scholars, some just regular soldiers, who worked to rescue the great art of Europe from the destruction of the war."

In the pictures, they looked like any old soldiers. But instead of holding guns, they held some of the world's most famous artworks. They posed next to sculptures, or in front of half-bombed churches, or with General Eisenhower as he reviewed what looked like hundreds of paintings.

"These guys were on the front lines, right behind the infantry. They drew maps of every European town showing the most important monuments— famous art museums, cathedrals, palaces—so our guys wouldn't bomb them by accident. And as soon as the Allies took a location away from the Nazis, the Monuments Men would go in and secure any endangered works of art. Make sure they were structurally sound, protected from further damage, or safe from looting."

"Looting by who? The townspeople? Or—," I gulped, "the American soldiers?"

"Both, I guess. But no one looted like the Nazis. The German leadership—Hitler, Goering, the whole lot of them—they were all art-obsessed, and they snatched up everything they could get their hands on. They stole from museums, estates, even private homes. And especially from the Jews that they shipped off to camps."

We'd covered a bit of the war in school: Pearl Harbor, D-Day, the concentration camps. I guess I never thought about great art in the midst of it all. But in the pages of the books Eddie laid out in front of me, I could see it. Stained-glass windows shattering. Historic buildings bombed. Paintings carefully packed and loaded out of a house as its occupants were hustled away at gunpoint.

"And then when the war was over, it fell to the Monuments Men to figure out what to do with all this stolen art. They established a collection point in Munich, and they spent the next few years cataloging everything and trying to send it back to where it came from." Eddie guided a snake-tatooed finger over Jack's archive file. "This says your grandfather worked there until nineteen forty-seven, when he was honorably discharged by his commanding officer."

I looked at the book's photographs again. Could that be Jack in the background, behind a Michelangelo? Or working to prop up a splintered cathedral? Maybe so, but then, every soldier looked the same in their regulation uniform and cap pulled low.

"I can't believe it," I mumbled. "He never said anything."

"That's a shame. Maybe you can track down someone in his division. You have all the info here, and some of these old-timers are even online now. Right, Stanley my man?" Eddie gave a fist pump to an oblivious elderly man hunched over a nearby computer terminal.

"Yeah. Yeah, that's a good idea. I'd like to know

more about," I cleared my throat, "what my grandfather was up to in those days."

"Here's a good place to start." Eddie slid the file
back over to me. "The record lists the commanding
officers by name. That's the CO who signed off on
your grandfather's discharge. A guy named," Eddie
peered at the papers, "Lydon Randolph."

Chapter Twelve

One summer, when I was around seven or eight, I was hanging around the museum, waiting for Jack to get off work so we could get an ice cream on our walk home. I was debating cherry versus chocolate-dipped when I turned the corner and saw Lydon and my grandfather talking. As they finished, Lydon pulled himself up tall and gave Jack a full military salute. Jack seemed mildly annoyed, but when he saw me over Lydon's shoulders, his face darkened. He looked back at his boss and shook his head almost imperceptibly. Lydon looked back at me and dropped the salute immediately, rumpling my hair as he walked away.

I thought nothing of it at the time. Jack had always shown a combination of grudging respect and open irritation around Lydon. "Even Michelangelo needed the Medicis," he'd sigh whenever I suggested he quit his job at the Met. He needed the job to support us and to support his painting. But it was like something bound him to Lydon despite their different values, positions, personalities. Like brothers.

Brothers in arms, I now knew.

I wished I could go back in time and see how this strange alliance began. And thanks to Lydon, in a way, I could. Jack's dense military file contained Lydon's field report, an incredible tale of adventure and audacity that showed just what united these two men, for the war and for the rest of their lives.

As Lydon recounted in those official typed pages, he and Jack made their way from France through Germany and into Austria, one step behind the advancing Allied forces the whole way. They drove their open jeep past grateful French survivors and weary inhabitants of bombed-out German villages, hoping that the woods weren't filled with soldiers intent on defending their land to the death. Mostly though, the German soldiers they encountered were all too happy to exchange their guns for a hot meal.

Their little jeep climbed up into the Austrian Alps, which had been happily spared the violence of war—except in one capacity. Under the surface of the peaceful alpine villages hid a treasure trove of Nazi loot. As the Nazis plundered Europe, they evacuated their choicest finds farther and farther into the mountains for protection. These mountains possessed salt mines that had provided the villagers a livelihood for centuries. They also provided perfectly calibrated temperature, light, and humidity levels: ideal for storing valuables. Their location miles under the surface of the earth protected their contents from bombing raids.

In just one salt mine in Merkers, an American fighting unit stumbled upon the Third Reich's entire gold reserve: row after row of gold bars and sacks of coins.

Military intelligence turned up evidence that Hitler's personal art collection had been deposited in a salt mine near Altaussee. But they also turned up Hitler's "Nero decree." As the German troops retreated, Hitler had issued a directive to destroy "all military, transportation, communications, industrial, and food-supply facilities, as well as all resources within the Reich which the enemy might use" before the Allies could reach them. The decree was mostly ignored by the fleeing Nazi officials. But some loyalists swore to fulfill Hitler's mission, no matter what the cost to their country or countrymen.

It was a race against time. When Jack and Lydon finally reached Altaussee, they immediately located the town's salt mine, plunging themselves down its long, dark tunnel, only to discover their worst fears had been realized. A quarter of a mile down, the tunnel was blocked with a wall of fallen rocks. The villagers had dynamited the mine.

But the locals were quick to explain their actions. Their district governor, a Nazi fanatic, had ordered eight boxes labeled "marble" loaded into the mine. Inside lay five-hundred-kilogram bombs, waiting to be detonated should the mine's contents fall into Allied hands. But the local miners didn't care about politics *or* art. They only knew that, with the mine destroyed, their livelihood would be destroyed with it.

In the dead of night, sympathetic guards looked the other way as the miners carefully removed the bombs and hid them in the forest. They then detonated a "palsy"—a controlled blast meant to seal off the mine's entrance so that no one else could get in.

Once they were assured that the Allies would protect the mine and its contents, the villagers were happy to help break through the rubble and open up the mine again. Inside, under the flickering light of lanterns, Jack and Lydon found an art collection that rivaled the Louvre, the Met, and London's National Gallery. Here was Van Eyck's *Ghent Altarpiece.* There was Michelangelo's sculpture, the *Bruges Madonna,* abandoned on an old mattress. Not one, but two Vermeers. And room upon room with racks upon racks containing thousands of other paintings, sculptures, drawings, and tapestries.

The men called in reinforcements, and for two weeks they worked to catalog the holdings. They calculated it would take a year to properly conserve, prepare, and move the artwork to the newly established processing center in Munich. But they didn't have a year. They had four days. Four days until the village was transferred into the Soviet Zone of Occupation—and Stalin's greedy hands.

The team worked sixteen-hour days, in relentless rain and fog, making do with the mine's nonfunctioning lights and antiquated mining trolley carts, thanking the slow-turning wheels of international politics for every delay in the handover process. In the end it took one month and eighty trucks to evacuate the mine. Jack and Lydon put themselves in the last truck, ready to unpack and reverse the whole process in Munich, where they would stay until all the artwork had found its way home again.

Two years later, they said their good-byes in

Munich. Though both were headed back to Manhattan, they must have believed their journey was at an end, as Lydon headed uptown to his new job at the Met, and Jack returned to his Spinney Lane studio. But just a few years later, Jack answered a want ad for a museum security guard. The men's fates were again entwined, and now I was tangled up in it, too.

The foyer seemed as dank and motionless as ever when I got home, but as I closed the door, I was surprised to hear the creaking of floorboards and overlapping voices above me: one high-pitched and wavering, another—a male voice—melodious and soothing. Two settings of Mrs. Tenpenny III's tea service sat abandoned in the parlor, the still-full cups of Earl Grey lending a hint of citrus to the room.

Clutching the manila envelope, I took the stairs two panicked steps at a time, following the voices all the way to Jack's studio. Bursting in, I found my mother sweating through her bathrobe as she struggled to make conversation with Lydon, who was using his cane to flip through Jack's canvases.

I'd never been so grateful for that Samsonite suitcase, currently hidden behind a pile of tarps in the far corner.

My mother looked so happy to see me she got tears in her eyes. "Theodora!" she heaved. "Mr. Randolph says he's a friend of Jack's? From the museum. He wanted a . . . a . . ."

"Well, just a visit to see how you two are holding up. I was in the neighborhood, so I thought I'd pop by—"

"I thought it was you knocking, that you'd forgotten your key," she whispered. "I wanted to tell you we're out of Darjeeling."

"I *told* you no more—" I hissed.

"I didn't realize how much you liked tea," Lydon broke in, "or I would have brought you this unusual Mariage Frères I picked up last time I was in Paris. But your mother has been such a delightful host, sharing her Earl Grey with me, giving me the grand tour."

"He wanted to see Jack's studio. I told him I was in the middle of an equation," she grabbed two fistfuls of her cornhusk hair, "but he didn't listen. He just came right up."

"I can take things from here." I took a firm hold of Mom's arm and steered her to the door. "You go back to work."

"You see, I'm in the middle of a very important derivation . . ." She continued her insistence all the way down the stairs.

"You should've waited for me." I turned back to Lydon, still hugging the envelope to my chest.

"Come now, your mother was quite welcoming and helpful for my purposes. All I need is a quick peek around." He resumed his hunt through the studio's contents without the pretense of a social call.

"This is private property. I should call the police right now. It's . . . it's . . . breaking and entering." No, that wasn't right. "Unlawful entry."

Lydon smiled placidly. "I don't think you will, my dear. Unless you'd like *them* to confiscate your precious stolen Raphael."

"It's not stolen." I snapped. *I think*, I added internally.

"I know," said Lydon as he moved on to the next stack of canvases. "At least, I know it's not stolen from the Met. After your eventful last visit, I checked the museum's records, and there are no Raphael paintings or sketches unaccounted for. So, on that front, it seems your grandfather is in the clear."

"Well, you said it yourself. There's nothing here that concerns the Met," I replied. "So what do you think you're doing here?"

"I believe my years of scholarship and service qualify me as an unofficial citizen-investigator." Lydon stopped to take in one of the larger abstracts. "I'd forgotten how sophisticated Jack's work was. Quite good, some of these."

I decided it was better to distract him with what I knew than to allow him to keep poking around. "Did you know his work before? Before the war?"

He looked at me a long time, weighing what to reveal himself. "No, I met him during the war." He turned back to the paintings. "I thought your grand-father didn't want you to know about all that."

"Well, I do now." I tossed the envelope to him, knocking over a Maxwell House can filled with paintbrushes.

He rescued the envelope from the clutter and glanced through its contents. "Well, this looks like the whole story here." He stopped and chuckled. "You even have my letter recommending him for a promotion. He turned it down, you know."

"Not quite the whole story. The file says he was on a classified mission at some point. Know anything about that?"

He leaned on his cane and shrugged. "No, I found Jack in a military hospital in France. He was recu-perating from a rather daring escape from a POW camp."

"Escape?"

"Yes. As I understand it, he managed to get out

somehow and walk back to the Allied line. I was looking for an assistant and heard there was an escapee nearby with art training. He'd sent word to Military Intelligence that he was 'bored' and looking for work to do." Lydon chuckled. "Bored, can you imagine?"

I thought back to our weekends at home, Jack a perpetual motion machine of chores. "Yeah, I can imagine."

"Anyway, he sounded like the kind of man I was looking for, and sure enough, he was itching to get back into the fray. He came on as my assistant, and it was just the two of us . . . well, liberating Europe's masterpieces." He tossed the envelope back to me. "And it seems your grandfather may have 'liberated' one painting in particular along the way."

"I don't know what you're talking about."

Lydon regarded me, then settled himself on a paint-splattered stool with his cane for support. "Let me tell you a story," he drawled. "In 1798 a Polish prince named Czartoryski traveled to Italy and returned with wagons full of Roman antiquities and two prized paintings: Leonardo da Vinci's *Lady with an Ermine*—a truly sublime work, if you haven't seen it—and a painting by Raphael. A painting believed to be a self-portrait."

I squirmed.

"The paintings," Lydon continued, "were displayed prominently as part of the family's museum until 1939, when the Germans invaded Poland. The Czartoryski family whisked away the most valuable works, bricking them up behind a wall at their family's country estate. Someone must have tipped off the Gestapo, as the items were found and seized almost immediately.

"The Leonardo and the Raphael were snatched up by the German governor sent to oversee the invasion of Poland. He used the paintings to decorate his personal apartments, but they were later sent on to Germany to become part of Hitler's personal collection."

Hitler's collection? In the salt mine?

"It seems Hans Frank managed to get the paintings back to Poland again for a spell, and after the war, the da Vinci and some other pieces surfaced. But to this day, eight hundred and forty-four of the Czartoryski artifacts are still missing—including the Raphael, which would be expected to fetch upward of one hundred million dollars in today's market."

Between the heat, the old paint fumes, and the factors of ten, I felt faint.

"There is some debate as to whether the painting

is a self-portrait or not." Lydon reached into his freshly pressed blazer and pulled out a folded square of paper. "Now, Miss Theodora, as our resident Raphael expert, what do you say? Does this man look familiar?"

I opened the paper with trembling hands.

An elegant young man of the Renaissance era regarded me, a sumptuous fur draped casually over his arm.

Alone. No Madonna or Child in sight.

Not my painting.

I exhaled and handed the paper back to Lydon. "Sorry, haven't seen him."

"Haven't you?" he said mildly, tucking the paper back in his pocket. "Well, yes, I expected that response. And perhaps you are even being honest with me. But I think we both know"—and here his eyes narrowed at the empty space above the mantelpiece, with its noticeably discolored outline, marking the spot where the painting had long hung—"that you're hiding *something*. Something that you believe to be a Raphael. And you may take it as a compliment that you are the only ten-year-old girl I know—"

"Thirteen," I corrected again.

"Thirteen, of course. The only thirteen-year-old girl I know who could actually spot a Raphael. I always told Jack you were our best curator-in-training."

Um, thank you?

"And if this is the case, the painting in question would be one of rare and immense value. A painting you are putting at untold risk. Chances are great that it is in fragile—probably already damaged—condition. Dear God, the temperature in here alone must be wreaking havoc on the structural integrity." He mopped his mostly bald head with his handkerchief. "And then there's the risk of theft—"

I folded my arms. "There's only one thief I'm worried about."

"It's not theft if it's a rescue." He looked around at the peeling wallpaper and defunct gas lamps. "A rescue operation as real and as urgent as any I performed in the war."

It's not theft if it's a rescue. The words rang in my ears, and I knew this had been my grandfather's justification, too. But the question still remained: a rescue from what?

The thing is, Jack had left it to me—not Lydon—to find out.

I raised myself up taller. "Get out of here," I said levelly. "Get out now. Or I yell 'Fire!' out the front window and bring the whole street running."

Lydon looked surprised and even a little impressed. "You don't need to make a fuss, my dear. A friend of mine at the club just happens to be a federal judge. I'll be back, but this time with a warrant in my hand and New York's Finest by my side. And then we will search this house from top to bottom until we find—I beg your pardon, *rescue*—whatever it is you're hiding."

I responded by walking over to the studio door and holding it open for his exit.

Lydon drew himself up and hobbled proudly past me, but when he stopped in the hallway, I was shocked to see tears in his eyes.

"Don't you see?" he whispered fiercely. "Don't you understand, you stupid girl? We're running out of time! *I'm* running out of time. A whole life spent waiting for this moment—for the mere *chance* at such a discovery—and you want to squander it, out of sheer stubbornness?" He grasped my wrist. "Would you really rob an old man of this?"

I pulled my arm away and ducked my head, too confused and ashamed to meet his gaze.

"I see. Well, after all, you are the granddaughter of a thief."

Chapter Thirteen

That night I slept with the painting under my bed.
I didn't like the idea of leaving the painting
in Jack's studio anymore, especially knowing that
my mom would serve the police tea and give them a
house tour. I was going to have to find the painting
another home.

Paparazzi or no paparazzi, I was going to have to
risk a visit to Bodhi's house.

The next morning, though, I was surprised to
find Spinney Lane abandoned except for a meter
maid enforcing alternate side parking. I walked
halfway up the block until I found 32 Spinney Lane,
with its matching façade, except that its bricks had
been restored until they were practically gleaming—not crumbling with chunks threatening to fall
on your head.

I rang the bell, and almost immediately a gelled young man wearing skinny jeans and a skinnier tie poked his head out the front door. "Yes?"

I pulled self-consciously at my 1970s gym shorts. "Is Bodhi home?"

The guy looked me up and down, then looked up and down the street. The lack of photographers seemed to make my entrance permissible, and he reluctantly opened the door. "Bodhi, you have a visitor," he called somewhere into the house's recesses as he drifted back to some task that required a laptop, a headset, and two cell phones.

If 18 Spinney Lane was like stepping into a time capsule, 32 Spinney Lane was like a time machine. The house had been hollowed out, stripped of its original details, the rabbit warren of rooms now gutted and ripped away. The ceiling above me had disappeared, sucked straight up into a fourth-floor skylight. The back of the house now consisted of a single, soaring wall of glass, making the house seem at one with the Asian rock garden out back. With white shiny floors melting into white walls, I felt like I was stepping into a giant eggshell.

Throughout this barren beehive buzzed a dozen staffers: operating the high-tech kitchen, barking orders into walkie-talkies, leading sun salutations in the garden. Given the high level of both activity and self-involvement, it was easy to see how Bodhi could wander in and out unnoticed.

"Hey!" Bodhi bounded down a floating staircase that clung impossibly to the wall. "What are you doing here? I was going to stop by your place later."

I bumped my knee on a near-invisible Lucite coffee table. "I decided to risk the paparazzi."

"Oh, yeah. They're all uptown today. My mom is doing a cameo on my dad's movie." Bodhi walked into the kitchen and high-fived a sushi chef as she squeezed past him. "Want something to eat?"

When didn't I?

"Daisuke, is the unagi-don ready yet?"

The chef grunted and jerked his head. Bodhi went over to what looked like a seamless wall of white and poked her finger in one spot, causing a door to spring open. She reached in and, pulling her shirt over her hands, withdrew two steaming black lacquered boxes. Another poke revealed the refrigerator, with Japanese pickles, seaweed salad, and two Cokes. Bodhi gathered it all on a tray and led the way back up the magic staircase.

Bodhi's room was a mirror of the house: a stark cube of neutral hues and tightly tucked sheets. Her desk was the only thing that resembled the Bodhi

I knew, covered in a jumble of expensive computer equipment and taped-up pictures of Raphael paintings, including printouts of the photos she'd snapped with her phone.

"So, what's up?" Bodhi sat down at the desk and stabbed her chopsticks into the hot bowl of roasted eel and rice. "I was looking into other paintings that have been X-rayed. Did you know they found a Ti— Tit—?" Bodhi furrowed her eyebrows.

"Titian. Pronounced Tih-shun."

"Okay, well, that guy painted a portrait of a woman with her son, and then someone else repainted the woman to be an angel. They found the woman again by X-ray. True story."

I picked up the other bowl and sat on the edge of her bed. "I was wondering if I could leave the painting here. For a few days."

Bodhi looked at me doubtfully. "Listen, I'd love to have the painting here. I was reading online about this blacklight test I want to try. But this house is crawling with people, and they're into everything. They clean my room twice a day, like a hotel. And they would notice something like that," she pointed her chopsticks at the printouts of the painting. "It doesn't exactly go with the decor."

"I guess you're right," I sighed. "But I don't know

what I'm going to do." I gave her the topline on Jack's military file, Lydon's visit, and his promise to return.

"Well, he's already poked around Jack's studio. So maybe that's the safest place to keep it? If he comes back, he'll probably start looking in the other parts of the house first. That would buy you time to move the painting. Maybe to the roof?"

"Maybe."

I nibbled a pickled plum and wondered how to navigate the fire escape with a hardside suitcase.

"So Lydon knows about the painting then?" said Bodhi.

"I don't think so. He knows there *is* a painting. And I think he knows where Jack got it."

"From—?"

"Hitler," I nodded.

"Do you think Jack's secret mission was to steal the painting from Hitler?" Bodhi's eyes glittered, and I could see her already writing the screenplay in her head.

"Maybe so." I hadn't put those two together until this moment. Had he been busted out of the camp by secret operatives with a plan to steal Hitler's favorite artworks? Didn't seem entirely plausible, but then, neither did anything else I'd found out in the last few weeks. "Before that, he was at a POW camp called Stalag IX-B, but the next three months on his file are classified."

"Stalag IX-B, huh?" Bodhi put the unagi-don aside and set to work at her computer. "Here it is. It's a POW camp in Germany. It held all kinds of Allied prisoners: American, French, Yugoslavian, Russian. And—oh."

"What?" I crossed the room to look over her shoulder. "What is it?"

"Just . . . It says here that it was one of the worst of all the camps. Worst conditions, I mean."

"Oh." I swallowed. "What else does it say?"

Bodhi scrolled down a bit. "Wait a minute. When was your grandfather missing?"

I thought back over the time line. "Let's see. Eddie said the Battle of the Bulge was right before Christmas. So the few months after that. January to March, maybe?"

"What year again?" asked Bodhi, already typing.

"Must be 1945."

Bodhi paused to scan a page, then turned back to me. "In that case, I think I know why your grandfather's file was classified.

Chapter Fourteen

An hour later, we were heading to Staten Island on the ferry (free).

Bodhi's computer skills had solved one mystery that day. Jack wasn't on a secret mission. He was in a secret hell.

But that hell wasn't so secret anymore. The information had been declassified at some point, but while the news found its way to the Internet, it must not have made it to the archives office that assembled Jack's file.

Apparently Jack had been transferred out of Stalag IX-B to a slave labor camp called Berga. Now, I'd read about Hitler's gas chambers, but I didn't know that the Nazis had another approach to killing prisoners: working them to death. Jack was one of 350 soldiers sent to Berga, and three months later, with the European war at an end, just 277 of the 350 men survived. They had been kept in appalling conditions and beaten, starved, worked until they dropped. The entire incident was deemed embarrassing to the U.S. victors, and on their discharge, the men were asked not to reveal the location or details of their internment.

It was hard enough discovering that Jack had been in the war in the first place. But it was near impossible to imagine my grandfather—a man who stood over six feet four in his eighties, who commanded the sidewalk with every stride, my hero, my protector—as one of the skeletal survivors who appeared on the web page. "It's not on his record," I protested as Bodhi pulled up the Wikipedia page on Berga. "It could still be a secret mission."

I remember that Bodhi looked at me with a hint of pity before she began silently typing on her computer again. A few minutes later, she hit print and said, "Well, there's one person who could clear this up."

And that's how we found ourselves on our way to the Sinai Retirement Home of Staten Island to meet Morris Novak, Private First Class, 28th Infantry

Division, and subject of the *New York Times* article Bodhi had found called "The Missing Men of Berga."

The old folks home was air-conditioned, but that was about the only thing inviting about it. The shuffling overweight nurses first glared at, then ignored us, while a janitor attempted to mop right under our feet. Abandoned wheelchairs (many still containing their frail passengers) lined the cinder-block hallways. Up until this point, I had thought of Jack's death as a tragic event. But it occurred to me that he'd probably have preferred it to this fluorescent-lit existence.

Bodhi played the role of a Novak grandchild convincingly enough to get Mr. Novak's room number. After taking something called a Shabbos elevator that stopped at each of twelve floors, we finally found room 1211. I knocked, and with no answer, pushed opened the door, hoping not to find any sponge baths in action.

The room was sunny and surprisingly homey, with plants and Mets pennants and a family photo collage that took up an entire wall. Bodhi and I tiptoed in and found a shriveled old man dozing in a wheelchair, a yarmulke bobby-pinned to his few remaining strands of white hair. A TV was tuned to championship surfing.

"Should we wake him up?" I whispered.

"Won't he wake up eventually?"

We waited.

He didn't wake up.

Bodhi broke the silence. "Is he alive?"

"Of course, he's alive." I didn't know one way or other, actually. "Go put your hand under his nose and see if you can feel his breath."

"He's got a tube in there!"

So he did. A tube snaked under his nose and over his shoulder to an oxygen tank on the floor.

"And why me, anyway?" Bodhi complained. "He's *your* granddad's friend."

"Who says? We don't even know if Jack was there—"

"Are you my great-grandchildren?"

Morris Novak was looking straight at us, his body still slumped in the chair but his chin lifted.

Bodhi and I waited for the other to speak. "No," I finally mumbled.

"Good. I'm pretty sure they're all boys. You're girls," he looked at Bodhi's khakis, "right?"

"Yes. I'm Theo—well, Theodora Tenpenny, and this is my friend Bodhi." We took turns shaking his limp hand. "We're here to ask about a friend."

"A friend?" He craned his neck and looked around the room. "I haven't seen any little girls around here, but I've been asleep."

"No, not a friend of ours. A friend of yours. My grandfather, Jack Tenpenny."

"Who?"

"Jack Tenpenny. He may have been in the war with you. Maybe somewhere called," I hated to say the name out loud, "Berga?"

His eyes grew dark, then brightened. "Oh, Jack! Yes, of course. Member of the Twenty-eighth. Haven't seen him since the war. How is the old man?"

"Dead."

"In the war?"

"No, last month."

"Well, that's not so bad. Every day aboveground is a good one, I say, and it sounds like he had almost as many days as me." He turned his wheelchair toward us and shakily motioned for us to have a seat.

"Turn that TV off, will you? I must have fallen asleep during the baseball. What was your name again, sweetheart?"

"Theo Tenpenny."

"Doesn't matter. I'll just forget it again. The old

short-term memory is shot." He scratched under his yarmulke. "But I can remember something that happened fifty years ago like it was yesterday."

Bodhi and I exchanged a look.

"That's why we're here." I switched off the surfing and pulled up a chair. "I just found out that Jack—that's Jack Tenpenny, remember?—was in the war. Maybe in the Berga camp. I'm wondering if you were there together."

"Well, sure. We were the only New Yorkers in our platoon, so we hit it off right away—even though he was a Yankees fan. I was a Dodgers fan, but when they left for Hollywood, I switched my allegiance to the Mets." He gestured to the pennants over his bed. "Do you know the score of the game, by the way?"

Bodhi checked her phone. "6–2, Red Sox. Tough luck, Mr. Novak."

He sighed. "Red Sox. How did their luck change all of a sudden? Hey, call me Mo, why don't you? My grandchildren do."

"So, Mo," I broke in, "you were with my grandfather when he was captured?"

"Yep. We got picked up trying to scout a better position for the Krauts to shell us."

"Were you sent to the POW camp then?"

"Yes, but that was Stalag IX-B. Nice accommodations there. Two hundred and fifty men to one drafty wooden barracks. Cracks an inch wide in the middle of January. And some of our boys without overcoats."

"No coats? How did you—"

"How did we stay warm? We didn't. We froze our *tuchuses* off. A couple of times a day we got some coffee made out of acorns and some 'grass soup,' we called it. And once a day we got a loaf of bread to share among four men: a paperweight made of flour and sawdust." He shuddered to remember it. "And you wouldn't believe the folks here who complain about the turkey tetrazzini."

"That sounds awful."

"The turkey tetrazzini? Nah, it's not so bad."

"No, the food at the camp."

"I tell you what was awful. That soup moved right through you. Two hundred and fifty guys with dysentery to one latrine. You couldn't even call it a latrine—just a hole in the ground. No baths. No showers. Not even toilet paper."

Now I shuddered. "But you didn't stay there?"

"No, not long. After about a month, the guards told our officers to turn over any Jews in the camp. Our guys told them where to go, of course. Word spread not to answer any questions about your religion. Some Jewish guys buried their dog tags. Our dog tags had an *H* on them for "Hebrew," you see. But then the guards started pulling anyone with a name that sounded Jewish or anyone who looked Jewish and moving them to a separate barracks. I went ahead and volunteered."

"You *volunteered?*"

"Yes, I did. I went in the army as a Jew. I fought for the right to be a Jew. If I was going to die, it was going to be as a Jew. And honestly I thought, how much worse could it be?"

"But Jack isn't—wasn't—Jewish. How did he end up with you?"

"The guards didn't have enough Jews to fill their quota, so they added in some troublemakers, and then just pulled men at random. I think Jack was one of the last recruits.

"They loaded us into boxcars. Five days with no heat, no food, no water. Only the snow that fell through the barred window.

"When we finally got to Berga, it looked like the same kind of setup we were used to, except there were these inmates at this camp; we called them 'zombies.' They looked like the walking dead. Like skeletons in pajamas. One of them wandered up to me and asked me a question. I answered him without even thinking about it, and then I realized we were speaking Yiddish. He was a Jew, like me. That's when I understood what was happening to the Jews of Europe. And what was going to happen to us."

"But isn't that why you enlisted?" I asked. "To fight for the Jews?"

"Bring me another oxygen tank, will you, honey?" Mo gestured to a collection of tanks in the corner, and I dragged one over. He labored to breathe as he made the switch. "We knew the Jews were being persecuted under the Nazis. We'd heard about some synagogues and businesses being burned. But we didn't know they were being slaughtered. We didn't know the plan was to work us to death.

"See, the Germans were getting desperate. They needed labor to work the mines up in the mountains there. That's where we came in. And those inmates in pajamas? Transfers from Auschwitz and Buchenwald. We didn't know about those places yet either.

"We were sent to these mines to break rocks, shovel debris, hand drill holes for dynamite. We carried rocks and dug holes with our bare, chapped, bleeding hands." Mo lifted his wrinkled hands and looked at them. "No gloves. No masks. Just breathing that dust filled with rock particles, in and out, ten hours a day. That's probably how I ended up with this thing." The oxygen tank gave off a clang as he flicked it with his finger. I realized that Jack's asthma wasn't something that kept him out of the war—it was something he'd brought back from it.

"If you moved too slow, you got a beating. If you dropped a load of rocks, you got a beating. If you stopped to catch your breath, you got a beating. Trouble was, we were on starvation rations. Even less food than we got at Stalag IX-B. None of us were in any condition to work at all, let alone hard labor. So you could count on a beating every day.

"We were all starving, all the time. But lucky for us, Jack and I got pulled up for kitchen duty. That's why we survived, I'm sure of it. The work was still tough: it took four men to pull these wagons with fifty-gallon vats of soup down a steep hill to the camp, and then back up the hill again. If you spilled any—"

"You got a beating," finished Bodhi.

"Right," said Mo, and he smiled a bit to see that we were actually listening. "But it was worth it. We got a bit of extra food here and there. And the best part was that, when we were pulling the cart, we could actually talk. Three of us, at least. The other guy only spoke Serbian."

"But the other three of you spoke English?"

"Yep. Mostly we talked about food. Meat loaf and

pot roast and pies and my grandma's kugel and Thanksgiving turkey and fresh-split watermelon. And coffee, real coffee." Mo seemed lost in a reverie, but then remembered something. "You girls want some cookies?" He produced a tin lined with waxed paper. "My niece brought rugelach. Cinnamon."

I could relate to Mo's food fantasies. Even with a belly full of beets, I thought constantly of the foods I wanted but couldn't have. I also understood Jack's lifelong obsession with our pantry's state of readiness. As I eagerly selected a flaky pastry, Bodhi elbowed me. "The painting."

I'd almost forgotten. "Did Jack ever talk about a painting?"

"No," said Mo as he helped himself to a rugelach. "No, that was Max."

"Who's Max?"

"Oh, I haven't mentioned Max?" Mo brushed the crumbs off his stubbled chin and clapped his hands together. "Max Trenczer. Everyone knew Max. He practically ran the camp."

"He was a guard?"

"No, he was a prisoner! A real *wunderkind*, this one. Polish by birth, I think, but he'd been some rich big shot in Paris before the war. He spoke a bunch of languages, all of them fluently. He would joke with the guards in perfect German, and they'd laugh and look the other way when he slipped extra bits of food in his pocket. He knew how to keep them happy, you see. If you had something of value—some of the prisoners still had watches or rings or even money somehow—you'd bring it to Max, and he'd trade it to the guards for extra food or cigarettes or clothing. He'd take a little off the top, sure, but he always made a fair trade."

"But he talked about a painting, you said?"

"Yeah. When we weren't talking food, Max and Jack talked art. Max had had a gallery in Paris before the Nazis got it. So Max and Jack talked about the paintings in his gallery, the ones he'd seen in all the big museums. And there was one in particular he talked about a lot." Mo's voice trailed off.

"Could you describe it?" I nudged gently.

"Sure I can." His voice caught in his throat, and he turned toward the window, with its view of a neighboring brick wall. "See, we were surrounded by ugliness. Up to our ankles in waste, surrounded by beatings and hunger. This was part of the Nazis' plan, do you see? To make even us believe that we had no place on this earth. But then the ugliness, the brutality would be pierced by this ray of beauty, and you'd think . . ."

He began again. "I remember in this painting there was a bird, a bird flying. And one day, as Max described it for the hundredth time, I heard a songbird up in the trees—maybe a lark? I don't know; I'm a city boy, I only know pigeons. But whatever it was, this bird sat and sang on that tree as the snow dripped in the sun, and there was spring in its song. Spring was coming, and I saw that if I could just make it till spring—well, the Allies were closing in. So every day, as I was pulling this wagon of slop, I would listen for that bird. And I would tell myself, 'Just one more day.'"

"A bird?" Now my voice caught in my throat. "Did the painting have a bird with a mother and child?"

"Yes, that was it." He looked back at me. "Did Jack tell you about it?"

I pressed on. "Did Max still have it? In the camp?"

"No, that was the thing. He'd traded it. When the Nazis rounded up the Jews in France, they said they'd just take the adults and leave the kids. But who knew how long that would last? Max had a little girl, about four or five years old. He was crazy about her. When he wasn't talking about the painting, he was talking about Anna. Anna this, Anna that. Anyway, when Max got word that he and his wife were being sent east, he promised the painting to some Nazi of-

ficer he knew—I'm telling you, he knew everyone—
if the guy could get his daughter to safety. There was
something about the painting that made him think
the Nazi would do anything to get his hands on it."

"Did Anna get out? Where did they send her?"

"He didn't know. Probably Spain. Maybe Swit-
zerland. Max and his wife were sent to Auschwitz,
where the wife was gassed immediately. He figured
out soon enough that his family back in Poland was
gone, too. Max was a big guy, so they kept him for
labor, and pretty soon he'd gotten himself transferred to Buchenwald and then to Berga. He could
make any trade, like I told you." Mo sighed. "But he
died without ever knowing if his daughter was safe."

"He died in the camp?"

"He died with your grandfather! Making that
escape almost got the rest of us killed."

"You were there when my grandfather escaped?"

Mo looked proud. "There? I knew all the plans!
Your grandfather knew the Americans were getting close. He figured that with his Aryan looks and
Max's German they could bluff their way through
the countryside, all the way to the Allied lines."

"Did you go with them?"

"They asked me to, but I said no. I thought I had
a better chance waiting it out in the camp kitchen

than in some German farmer's barn. Max got his hands on a couple of Nazi uniforms, and every night after roll call, they'd put them on under their clothes. The guards turned off the electricity during the night air raids, you see, and Max and Jack would be able to crawl under the electrified fence and slip into the forest.

"So finally one night there was a raid, and they ran for the fence as soon as the guards cut the juice. But Max got his jacket caught on the wire, and by the time the lights went up, there he was. And it was all over. One shot."

"But Jack got away?"

"He got away, although how, I'll never know. They sent guards and dogs out after him. Of course, the rest of us at camp bore the brunt of his punishment. They cut our rations in half for the next week."

"Cut your rations? In *half?*" Bodhi sputtered. "But half of nothing is—"

"Bubkes. And when the Allied troops started to close in, the guards packed us up and marched us east for two weeks. By the time the Americans finally caught up with us, I weighed a hundred pounds." Mo chuckled softly. "And to think my mom always said I was too skinny."

I gasped. At my last physical I'd weighed a little

over a hundred pounds. Me, a thirteen-year-old girl. Not a soldier keeping the world safe for democracy.

"What did your mom say when she saw you?"

"The docs fixed me up before shipping me home, and I never talked about it. At the hospital, they made me sign a piece of paper, saying that I couldn't talk about Berga. For 'wartime and peacetime security,'" Mo shook his head bitterly. "Even then I knew that was a load of bunk. They just didn't want any bad blood while they tried to lure all of Germany's best scientists to the States."

"You sound angry." And it was no surprise. Knowing what happened at Berga, I understood why Jack stole back a painting from his friend's killers and hid it away for years. "I think my grandfather felt the same way."

"Angry? Nah. I don't believe in anger. Only revenge."

"How did you get your revenge?" asked Bodhi, looking around the room for another painting, waiting to be discovered.

Mo gestured with one shaky hand to the photos that covered his wall: a patchwork quilt of weddings, bar mitzvahs, and family reunions; generations of baby pictures mixed in with vacation photos and more than one snapshot of someone receiving a plaque or presenting a giant check. "Genesis Fifteen. 'Look up at the heavens and count the stars. So shall be your descendants.'" Mo smiled. "That's enough revenge for me."

Bodhi and I were quiet on the ferry back to Manhattan. Partly, I think, we were enjoying the salty harbor air on that hot afternoon. But as the Statue of Liberty approached, we both lingered at the railing as she passed by.

"So the painting belonged to that guy, Max?" Bodhi finally broke in.

I nodded.

"How did it end up with Hitler?"

"I'm guessing that the Nazi officer, whoever he was, gave it to Hitler. Or maybe gave it to his boss, who gave it to his boss, all the way up the line. That book on the Monuments Men said that all the Nazis collected art, and they used it to get promoted and stuff."

"So the painting *really* belongs to Max."

I thought about it. "I don't know. He did trade it, fair and square."

"It's only fair and square if Anna made it out alive."

"Who?"

"Anna. Max's daughter."

"Oh, right."

Bodhi tapped my head with her finger. "You know, you should really be writing this stuff down."

She was right. I dug in my sweater bag for a pen and some old homework pages.

"Okay," I scratched, "Max was at Berga—"

"And Auschwitz and Buchenwald, too," Bodhi added.

"Okay . . . Buchenwald . . . got it. March–April 1945, Max, what was his last name?"

"Trenczer?"

"Right, Max Trenczer, daughter Anna Trenczer . . ."

"I wonder if she did make it out. I wonder if there's an Anna Trenczer out there somewhere." Bodhi hung her shoulders over the railing, her braids dangling, her hands reaching to catch the boat's spray. "We should try and find her before it's too late."

I looked up from my notes. "Wait . . . what?"

Bodhi stood up and raised her voice over the drone of the engine. "I said, we should find Anna Trenczer before it's too late."

Anna Trenczer. Before it's too late.

Not "and a treasure." Anna Trenczer.

It's just what my grandfather asked of me in his dying moments. To find his letter—and Anna Trenczer—before it's too late.

Chapter Fifteen

I didn't exactly race out and search the four corners of the earth for Anna Trenczer. I sat with this revelation and mulled it over for a day or two.

Okay, it was five.

I'm not proud of this. What I was, as Jack would say, was cheesed off.

Nothing against Miss Trenczer. I'm sure she was a lovely girl, or as lovely as a four-year-old could be. No, my growing sense of injustice was reserved for my own grandfather.

Here we have a painting that Jack sat on for sixty years. Did he try and sell it? No. Did he leave me its sales history or background so that I could sell it? No. Did he turn it in himself and claim some kind of reward? No. Did he at least leave me with a clear record of this girl's name and story so that I could find her, if that's what he cared about so darn much? No.

Instead, he promises me a "treasure," but leaves me with a gurgled mission to find some girl he's never met and give *her* the painting. Her.

So rather than embarking on the Great Search for Anna Trenczer, I spent the next few days dedicating myself to the house. If I couldn't find a treasure, I'd have to do the hard work of making our money—and our house—last.

I brought a panicked determination to my chores. I canned, I pickled, I jellied. I snaked the kitchen sink. I plunged the upstairs toilet. I hauled the remaining Tenpenny silver—now just a jumble of obsolete tongs and prongs—to a pawnshop, netting a much-needed $78. I even ransacked Jack's armoire, the one blocking the leftover connecting door between our house and Madame Dumont's, for loose change. (Jack pushed it there after Madame Dumont complained about his loud snoring. I think he really believed she was going to sneak in and smother him in his sleep.)

All the while, my mom scritch-scratched away on her legal pads.

With one ear always listening for the door, I worked through my to-do list. I also nurtured a fantasy where I'd meet Lydon, the cops, and their warrant at the door with the painting: "It belongs to someone named Anna Trenczer. Good luck finding her." Slam.

As it turns out, the only raps at the door came from Bodhi. But I skulked around with the curtains drawn, deliberately avoiding her knocks and notes.

Tuesday morning I found a slip of paper shoved through the mail slot: *Googling 'Anna Trenczer'/'Anna Trencher', but found 0. Prbly married, chgd name. Wd Eddie know how 2 find out? Meet @ library today @ 12:00. B.*

I spent the day taking inventory on the pantry (beans getting low) and doing another round of canning. On Wednesday I got this note: *Where r u? Eddie gave me some books on Holocaust. Also, he has a friend who can help us. Y DON'T U HAVE A PHONE?!?*

Thursday I got two notes: *R u trapped under a chiffarobe?* and *?????????????*.

Friday morning was particularly stifling, and when I looked in the mirror I saw that I was starting to get crazy eyes like that lady in the park who wears underwear over her clothes. It was time to leave the house.

The day wasn't good for anything besides the city pool, so I put on my mom's old neon bathing suit and a cover-up I'd made out of an old towel. With the garden tended, my mother's tea tray by her door, and a lunch of hard-boiled eggs and green beans in my sweater bag, I headed out the front door feeling quite self-sufficient.

Bodhi was waiting for me on the front stoop.

She brushed the paint chips off the back of her khakis as she stood up. "Finally."

"Oh, hi. There you are," I chirped.

"No, there *you* are. Why have you been avoiding me?"

"I haven't been avoiding—"

"—me, yes you have." Bodhi blocked my way, her arms folded.

"I've been busy," I sniffed. "Some of us have chores, you know. Some of us don't have a team of assistants to run our lives."

Bodhi regarded me with more amusement than anger. "I think you're the one who wants a team of assistants. But I'm not doing this alone."

"What alone? I didn't ask you to do anything."

"What do you think I'm doing? Finding this girl, this Anna Trenczer."

Bodhi's big brown eyes were fixed on me, and I looked away. "I'm not sure I want to find her."

I squeezed past Bodhi and headed down the sidewalk.

"Don't want to find her?" Bodhi trotted alongside me. "Isn't that what your grandfather asked you to do? There's this girl out there—well, a woman now—waiting for her painting. You're just going to hold on to it?"

"Isn't that what Jack did? Why should I do anything different?"

We rounded Seventh Avenue, my course fixed on the pool.

"Listen," I huffed, "I've lost my grandfather. I've lost the painting that I looked at every morning of my life. I've lost the hidden stash of treasure—if there ever even was one—that was promised to me. And if I give this painting away, I'll lose the last thing—it turns out the only thing—my grandfather left me." I stopped in the middle of the sidewalk. "I'm not losing any more."

Bodhi looked baffled. "You're crazy. Yeah, you've lost some things, but you've found so much. You've found this beautiful painting. You've found a whole side of your grandfather you never knew existed. You've found all this history and all these people and all their stories."

She smiled shyly.

"And you've found a friend. So have I." Bodhi linked her arm in mine like a character in a Nancy Drew book. "This is turning into the best summer

I've ever had. And that includes the summer I spent snowboarding in Argentina."

"Why, girls, what fun. I was just thinking of you."

We looked up to see a familiar figure in black waddling toward us. Reverend Cecily still wore her Birkenstocks, but now with a combination of black Bermuda shorts and shirt with a priest's collar.

"How goes your mystery? Was my friend Gus of any help?"

"Who?"

"Augustus Garvey. My parishioner at Cadwalader's."

If I had known he went by Gus, I might not have been so intimidated. "Not exactly."

"Oh, that's a shame. This painting has gotten under my skin, you know. There's something about it, isn't there? One look, and it just takes hold."

"That's just what I was saying to Theo here." Bodhi stuck out her tongue at me.

"Well, I was just mulling it over the other day," Reverend Cecily rummaged around a satchel she carried and produced a folded up slip of paper, "I went back to the poem and found an alternate reading. There's something about this idea of Raphael."

Bodhi and I exchanged looks. In all the excitement around Nazis and secret missions and missing girls, I'd almost forgotten about the painting itself.

"Raphael, huh?" I reached out my hand. "Well, anything's possible. Maybe I could look at those notes?"

"Of course." She pressed the paper into my open hand. "But you must promise me to come back and report all your findings. I have become quite entranced by this painting."

"Will do. Well, thanks, Reverend Cecily."

"Not at all." She gave my shoulder a squeeze and waddled away down Seventh Avenue.

Bodhi blocked my way on the sidewalk again. "She's right. And you know she's right."

"Who's right?" A shadow fell over me as a hulking figure drew near enough to block out the sun. It was Eddie. He flipped his mirrored sunglasses on top of his shaved head. "I thought we were meeting at the diner."

"We were. But this one's having second thoughts."

"Who's meeting at the diner?" I looked back and forth between them.

"We are. You are. That's why I came by your house. Eddie found us a lead."

"Well, not a lead. A friend. Well, not a friend. Although, you know, we're friend*ly*, but not friend-friends," Eddie blushed. "A classmate. From my Library Science degree. Anyway, she works nearby, and she said she can help you track down this missing girl."

I looked at Bodhi. "You told him?"

"Why not?"

"Why not? Because—" I must have been yelling, because even a hipster in headphones looked up. "Because this is *my* painting, *my* mystery, and *my* business. And it's *my* decision whether or not to finish it."

"Oh, hello, Miss Theo." The smell of roasted vanilla floated over me, and I turned around to see Sanjiv pushing his cart past us. "I was thinking about your dilemma. Latex. It must be latex paint, I think. I have some research to show you."

Bodhi put her arm around my shoulder.

"Sorry, Theo. It's bigger than the both of us now."

Chapter Sixteen

Eddie's friend worked at the Center of Jewish History, a high-tech research consortium built out of five different organizations across six conjoined buildings. We were metal-detected, registered, photographed, reregistered, and finally admitted to the central reading room. Between my towel-dress, Bodhi's uniform, and Eddie's tattoos, we didn't exactly blend in among the scholars bent over their Talmuds and laptops.

Eddie's friend Goldie jumped in immediately, dismissing any pleasantries. "Okay, Eddie, I got your e-mail. Who exactly are we looking for?" she asked, pushing up her headband and positioning herself at a terminal behind the long reception desk. She spoke with a slight accent, sort of Brooklyn by way of

Poland, and her voice sailed through the library like a deli order.

"It's for me," I said, pulling my towel-dress up deeper into my armpits. Next to Goldie's conservative black stockings and long sleeves, I felt half naked—which technically I was. "We're looking for a girl, Anna Trenczer. Well, a woman now."

"If she's alive at all," added Bodhi.

Goldie nodded, unfazed. "Okay, we'll start with the obvious sources first. Yad Vashem—"

"That's the Holocaust museum in Israel," Eddie cut in for our benefit.

Goldie's focus never left the computer screen. "Yad Vashem has the world's most comprehensive online database of Holocaust victims . . . and . . ." she typed and hit enter, typed and hit enter, ". . . they're not showing anything for Anna Trenczer—"

I leaned over the desk. "It could be spelled with -C-Z-E-R, but also with -C-H-E-R, or possibly—"

"Obviously. I already allowed for phonetic matches." Goldie rolled her eyes at Eddie as if to say, "Amateurs."

"Oh." I must have sounded disappointed, because Goldie stopped and looked at me. "Look now, don't panic. First of all, this is maybe good news. This database contains only the names of the deceased, not survivors. So if Anna Trenczer is not here, then maybe she survived."

"So . . . it's good news?" asked Bodhi.

"Well, you have to remember: even the Yad Vashem site only contains about two-thirds of the Jewish victims. That's around two million people unaccounted for."

Two million people. Vanished. With no record of their life or death.

Goldie continued. "For survivors, the best place to look is—

"—the U.S. Holocaust Museum database. They have a Survivors Registry, plus they're an excellent source of recorded oral histories and survivor testimonies." Eddie beamed.

Goldie looked annoyed. "Yes, I know. Quit interrupting me!"

Bodhi elbowed Eddie in the ribs. "Dude," she whispered, "play it cool."

More typing from Goldie. "The problem there, of course, is that Anna Trenczer would have had to register herself." Not surprisingly, she hadn't.

I started to sigh, but Goldie stopped me with one look. "Listen, this is not one-stop shopping, you know? Even if we find something, you have to remember that the files are not entirely accurate. Just last week a guy comes in and says, 'So, I'm dead and no one told me?' His cousin had submitted testimony that he died in a camp. So remember: we have to cross-check many, many sources."

The sign above Goldie read NO FOOD AND DRINK. My stomach rumbled.

"No Anna Trenczer-Trencher-Trencer-Trenser in the refugee organizations. None on the orphan lists." Goldie flitted from terminal to bookshelf to file cabinet, an elfin information powerhouse. "Nothing with European Jewish Children's Aid. No Holocaust restitution claims filed . . ." She stopped at the keyboard again. "You said she was last seen in France?"

"Yes, she—"

Goldie had already ping-ponged her way to the website for Mémorial de la Shoah, the research center in Paris. "Got it. See?" She turned the terminal our way, and we all three leaned in to get a better look.

There was the whole Trenczer family, their tragic fate boiled down to a few lines on a computer screen.

Monsieur TRENCZER Maxim né le 26/05/1909 à CRACOVIE. Interné à Drancy de 17/07/1942. Déporté à Auschwitz par le convoi n° 17 au départ de Drancy le 10/08/1942. De profession propriétaire de la galerie.

Madame TRENCZER Éva née le 22/04/1911 à

CRACOVIE. *Internée à Drancy de 17/07/1942. Déportée à Auschwitz par le convoi n° 17 au départ de Drancy le 10/08/1942.*

Mademoiselle TRENCZER Anna née le 3/10/1937 à PARIS. Internée à Drancy de 17/07/1942.

"I only read German and Yiddish," said Goldie. "Anyone read French?"

Bodhi reached for her translation app, but I put my hand over her phone. "No."

"I do!" jumped in Eddie. "I mean," he said, with a mighty effort at restraint, "I might, y'know, know a little."

"Okay then. Let's see what you've got." Goldie turned the computer screen toward him.

"It's showing us the family's internment and deportation," Eddie began. Was he sucking in his gut? "Says here the dad, Max, was born in Kraków in oh nine, but was held at Drancy—meaning he was living in Paris—until he was deported. Sent to Auschwitz on the train convoy numbered seventeen. His wife, Eva, too; same transport."

Goldie looked approvingly at Eddie, then moved to another terminal where she accessed another database. "Eva and Max do pop up on the Yad Vashem databases. Eva's death at Auschwitz confirmed shortly after the convoy arrived. Max transferred out to Buchenwald, then Berga-an-der-Elster, died March 7, 1945." She came back to our terminal and tapped the screen. "This is good news."

I blinked. "In what possible way is any of this awful story good?"

"Because it confirms everything you've told me so far, which means your sources are credible. And look at Anna's file again. What's missing?"

Mademoiselle TRENCZER Anna née le 23/10/1937 à PARIS. Internée à Drancy de 17/07/1942. Anna Trenczer, born in Paris, interned at Drancy . . . that's all.

"There's no deportation date," said Eddie. "She was never sent out of the camp."

"Right," said Goldie, and I think she may have even smiled. "It's promising."

"But it doesn't tell us anything new," complained Bodhi. "We still don't know what happened to her."

"What time is it?" Goldie asked.

Eddie held out his watch. "Eleven forty-two!"

"There might be time . . ." Goldie trailed off as she exited through a small door behind her.

We waited there for ten or fifteen minutes. Bodhi gave Eddie more tips on playing-hard-to-get. Eddie responded by peering through the door compulsively every few seconds.

Goldie finally re-emerged with an enormous book in her arms and heaved it on the counter. "Found her."

"You found her? Where is she?" As the words left my mouth, I didn't know whether to feel happy or sad.

"Well. Kind of." Goldie readjusted her headband again and started paging through the book. "I called a colleague at the Mémorial de la Shoah."

"Of course," Eddie nodded. "In Paris."

"Yes. And I was lucky to catch him before he went home. Anyway, they have access there to more of the Drancy documents. And Jean-Paul—that's my colleague—found Anna Trenczer's file. He said she was signed out of the camp on," Goldie stopped to consult her notes, "August 28, 1942, by a Nazi officer named Hans Brandt."

"Signed out?" It made it sound as if he was taking her to a dental appointment. "Where did he take her?"

"I don't know. And we can't ask Herr Brandt because he committed suicide in nineteen forty-five while awaiting trial for war crimes."

"Hans Brandt." Eddie stroked his goatee. "That sounds familiar to me. Was he—"

"Yes, the man overseeing the deportations. He's also known by his moniker, the Paris Executioner."

"Oh, yes, now I remember. Brandt features heavily in Beliveau's work on French collaboration and the Vichy Regime. Fascinating reading."

Goldie's eyes lit up, and I swear I saw her eyelashes bat. "I know, isn't it? Well, if you liked Beliveau, you should read Brunner's book on the postwar—"

"Excuse me. Did you really just say 'the Paris Executioner'?" Bodhi broke in. "Um, that doesn't sound good."

"No," Goldie turned back to us, "it doesn't. But there's one bit of good news. Jean-Paul also reminded me of a book in our collection. A compilation of sixty-five thousand identity cards from a nineteen forty-one census of Jews living in France. I've got it here." She flipped past one black-and-white face after another, each attached to an official-looking card. "It may not help us find Anna, but it should give us—oh! Here." Goldie pointed to a photo in the middle of the book. "There she is. That's Anna Trenczer."

We looked, and at the same moment, we gasped. Because, in the midst of page after page of terrified, terrorized faces, here was the face of blissful ignorance. With her neatly combed bob and toothy grin, this was a girl who knew nothing of the reasons behind her latest portrait. Her smile said: And why wouldn't you want to snap my picture? Will we get ice cream afterward?

The idea of this girl left in the hands of the Paris Executioner was sickening.

"It's nice to have a face to the name," Bodhi said, "but does it buy us anything? I mean, does it get us any closer to finding Anna?"

"No," said Goldie bluntly. "This is the 'before.' This," she pointed to the database still up on the computer screen, "is the 'after.' And the 'after' is going to take a lot more work."

"More work for . . ." I looked at Goldie hopefully.

"For you. Or for someone you hire; there are archivists who take on cases like these for a fee." She saw my face fall, and her eyes seemed to take in the scruffiness of our ragtag group.

Eddie leaned his elbows on the counter. "It wouldn't be the same working with anyone else."

Goldie ducked her chin shyly. "Well, *maybe* I could do a bit more digging. But I have to warn you: Survivors of the Holocaust are much harder to track down than the victims. The survivors who have died since the war are even harder; we don't have any wartime death records to go on, and they're no longer in any telephone books or electronic databases."

Goldie looked back and forth at our expectant faces, then sighed and glanced at her notes once more. "There is one thing. It's Hans Brandt. We know he was ruthlessly efficient at rounding up Jews, but he was also a devout Roman Catholic."

"I wouldn't call him exactly devout," muttered Bodhi.

"Trust me, these Nazis were pretty inconsistent, morality-wise. Anyway, Brandt sent Jews, Gypsies, dissidents—all kinds of people to the camps—but he left the convents and monasteries in his districts pretty much alone. It's possible . . ." She tapped her notes with a pen. "And if they still had the baptismal certificates . . ."

"Baptismal certificates?" I shook my head. "What does that have to do with—"

Goldie, her mind now commandeered by her latest theory, reached for another book and waved us away with her hands. Bodhi and I crept away to re-collect our bags from the storage lockers.

"Eddie, you coming?"

But Eddie didn't hear us. He was bent over the book with Goldie, their heads almost touching. More volumes towered just beyond Goldie's elbow. This might take all afternoon.

Chapter Seventeen

While Goldie pursued her mysterious lead and Lydon plotted his warrant, Bodhi and I had nothing to do but wait. We regrouped the next day in Jack's studio, guarding the painting while we sipped un-iced tea (really, just the leftover morning's tea served lukewarm in jelly jars).

It was clear we were at a crossroads—but we didn't even know which directions the signs pointed.

"To wit:—" I launched in.

"To *what?*" Bodhi interrupted.

"To wit," I said. "It means, thusly—"

Bodhi rolled her eyes. "Oh jeez, just talk like a normal person for once and not like an eighty-year-old in your old lady slip."

"Fine, okay," I said, crossing my arms over my grandmother's repurposed negligee (which I had thought made a nice sundress). "Here's what we know. Anna Trenczer is probably—let's face it—dead. Even if she survived the camp, it's not likely she survived the Paris Executioner. And we know her parents are dead, and most likely, all of her family members."

"We don't know that actually," mused Bodhi. "There could be some long, lost cousin out there."

"Yes," I admitted, "but we won't find them without hiring an archivist, like Goldie said."

"True dat," nodded Bodhi.

"Okay, I'll stop talking like an old lady if you stop impersonating rap stars."

"Hip-hop artists," Bodhi corrected. I gave her a look, after which she said nothing but made an okay sign.

"We also know that the painting is stolen."

"With no authentication."

"Or documentation. So I can't sell it."

"And if you can't find Anna, you can't return it."

"So what was the point?" I clenched my jar of tea. "Jack must've known that I had no chance of finding Anna Trenczer. So why leave me with this great big mystery? Why shouldn't I just give the stupid painting to Lydon?"

"I don't know, Theo," said Bodhi. "Maybe you should."

We sat with that sign on the crossroads, attempting to dismantle the mental roadblock that kept us from admitting defeat.

Bodhi finally spoke. "There is one thing that Goldie said that's been bothering me."

"Just one?"

"Okay, there were a lot of things that were . . . disturbing. But only one that doesn't make sense. The Nazi officer—he signed Anna out of the camp, right?"

"The Paris Executioner? Seems so."

Bodhi started pacing the room. "Well, why? If he wanted her to die, he could've just left her there."

"He needed the painting. She had it."

"So?" Bodhi stopped in front of me. "He could have gone to the camp—or sent some underling, for that matter—grabbed the painting, kicked her back inside."

Slowly it dawned on me. "But he signed her out . . ."

"Exactly. I mean, if the Executioner wanted to kill her, it would have been a lot easier to just leave her at the camp and let the system do the dirty work."

"So do you think he got her to safety?"

Bodhi spoke tentatively. "I think maybe he did."

"And maybe—"

I was interrupted by a banging on the front door that carried all the way up the stairs. The kind of insistent banging that's only produced by a fist.

Bodhi and I ran to the small front window of Jack's studio that overlooked the street, where a squad car was double-parked. Below, on the stoop, stood at least three men in police uniforms. Plus an older man in a seersucker suit.

I knew in that instant that, whatever happened to the painting, it was not going to leave this house by force. Not this way.

I turned to Bodhi. "Do you think we can wait them out?" I remembered Lydon's last threats. "They probably have a warrant."

Bodhi shook her head. "I dunno. My dad has been in a couple of cop movies, and I think they can bust their way in if they have a warrant."

I started moving paintings around the studio, looking for a hiding place.

"They're going to search the whole house, you know," said Bodhi.

I stopped with my arms full of unfinished canvases. "I know."

"What about behind the house? In the chicken coop?"

"That's not a bad idea." I looked out the front window again. "But they'll see us coming down the stairs. Through the glass of the front door."

"What about the basement?"

"Still have to go down the front stairs."

"Theo? Theo, are you up there? There's someone at the door."

My mom's reedy voice floated through the house.

"Shhhhh, Mom," I hissed. "I'll be down in a minute."

Turning back to Bodhi, I said, "We've got to find somewhere to stash this before—"

Lydon's muffled voice drifted through the door and all the way up the staircase. "Theodora, we know you're in there. I have a warrant here, and these police officers have every right to break your door down if you don't open it of your own accord. Be a good girl now."

"Before that," I finished.

Bodhi furrowed her brow. "Don't you have any secret rooms or passageways or something in this old house?"

One dim, 30-watt lightbulb went off in my brain. "It's a risk," I muttered. "But she would be at the shop now. And I could get it back before she gets home . . ." I thrust the painting into Bodhi's arms and headed down the stairs to the second floor, calling over my shoulder, "Wait at the top of the stairs. I've got to talk to my mom."

My mom was hovering on the second floor landing in her bathrobe. "Theo, aren't you going to answer it?" She looked worried. "They seem impatient."

"Mom, look me in the eyes." She made a few efforts, her eyes finally landing on my shoulder. Close enough. "Mom, I need you to do something very important. That's Lydon Randolph downstairs with some friends of his. They are coming to see me, but I'm not ready for them yet. I need you to make them some tea."

"Tea?" She blinked rapidly. "Why me?"

"Because I have to get something ready for them, and you're the only one I can trust to know the right kind of tea to serve."

My mom looked momentarily confused, then proud. "Lydon and his friends? What kind of friends?"

"Police officers."

She stood up a bit taller. "Oh, well, that's easy. Something strong and bracing. Lapsang Souchong. I could do that, I suppose." She wrapped her bathrobe around her tighter. "And the kettle is—"

"On the stove."

"And the Lapsang—"

"On the windowsill in the yellow tin." I pushed her in the direction of the stairs. "Oh! And they are really interested in—what's that thing you're working on?"

"Fermat's Last Theorem?"

"Yes! That's why they're here. To hear about that."

As my mother tripped downstairs like a girl with a gentleman caller, I waved Bodhi and the painting down to the second floor and pulled her into Jack's old bedroom. We closed his door just as I heard my mother greeting Lydon and his merry band.

Jack's scent had faded, but at that moment, it felt overwhelming: paint, turpentine, Old Spice, the smoke of his one Saturday night cigarette. The furniture was just as he'd left it, too: a grand Victorian bedroom set made up with spartan Army blankets. It occurred to me for the first time that they were military issue, brought home from the war.

"How much time can your mom really buy us?" asked Bodhi.

"They won't start here. They'll start poking around downstairs, or go right to the studio. We only need five minutes."

"But they'll look in here eventually."

"Yes," I agreed, "but they won't look in *here*." I gestured dramatically to the heavy armoire that domi-
nated Jack's room.

"Of course they'll look in there. They'll search
every closet." Bodhi shook her head. "What's wrong
with you?"

"No, not in *there*." I braced my back against the
side of the armoire. "Listen, just put the painting
down and grab hold of the other side. And help me
move this as quietly as you can."

The armoire weighed twice as much as any other
piece of furniture in the house, but we managed
to slide it along the floor an inch at a time, hoping
the groans and creaks would be lost in the confused
conversation I heard downstairs. As predicted, the
combination of Mom's meandering thoughts and
Lydon's attempts to appear chivalrous in front of
the cops was buying us the time we needed.

Finally the armoire had been heaved aside, revealing the door that led directly into 20 Spinney
Lane, home of Madame Dumont and brief dwelling
place of the first Grandmama Tenpenny.

I said a silent prayer that Madame Dumont was
indeed at the shop, turned the knob, and pushed
my shoulder against the door. It flew open with sur-

prising ease, and I tumbled on the floor after it.

No Madame Dumont here. I was surrounded by blackness and the smell of mothballs, a jungle of hanging fabric and plastic wrap entangling me from all sides. It turns out Jack didn't have to worry about a lurking Madame Dumont all those years. She, or some earlier occupant, had built a closet in front of the door.

"Are you okay?" asked Bodhi, her head haloed by the light of Jack's room.

I swatted away something woolen. "Yes, fine. Give me the painting."

Bodhi stepped into the dark closet and placed the painting in my arms. "Better hurry. I just heard them heading up to the studio."

I left the painting right there on the floor and hopped back into Jack's room, where we reversed the moving process and planted the armoire right back where we'd found it.

By the time Lydon and his men had finished ransacking the rest of the house, Bodhi and I were sitting in the parlor with my mother, drinking Lapsang Souchong and listening to her rattle on about Whoever's Last Theorem.

"Find anything good?" Bodhi inquired sweetly

as the men reentered the parlor, wiping their fore-heads on their shirtsleeves.

Lydon's tired face reminded me of an old cartoon character who always complained about "those med-dling kids." "Despite an incriminating amount of noise and disruption from your upper floors, no, we did not." He loosened his tie. "Care to tell us any-thing, girls?"

"Not really," I said, sipping my tea.

He turned to the officers who looked hot and bored. "It's clear they have it. Somewhere in this house. Maybe in the walls or some hidden entrance. We need to get some kind of equipment to open up the walls. Or one of those detectors that locate hollow spots. Or—"

The cops exchanged glances that said that this job was not going to get them any closer to making detective. The most senior looking one spoke up: "That's going to require a different kind of warrant than the one you got, sir."

"What? Why? My good friend, Harry—Judge Harold Greenbaum to you—said all the paperwork was in order."

"Mr. Randolph, I think we'd better take this out-side."

Lydon drew up his shoulders. "Yes, I think we'd better.

My mother watched the men go, shaking her head. "They didn't seem to know much at all about algebraic number theory," she said, and shuffled her way back to her room.

As soon as she left, Bodhi turned to me, her eyes ablaze. "Upstairs, and quick!"

We tiptoed past the front door and up the stairs, the men too immersed in their debate to notice us, back up to Jack's room. "Do you have a fire escape?" asked Bodhi.

"Sure, but it just leads out to the backyard. And there isn't any way to get out of the yard again."

"What about the roof? Couldn't you climb up to the roof from the fire escape outside Jack's studio?"

"Maybe. But not with a painting under my arm."

"Then I'll climb up. You hand me the painting. Then I walk over the rooftops to my house, slip our bodyguard twenty dollars—well, maybe fifty dollars—not to tell my parents, and climb down my own fire escape. Like Robert DeNiro in *Godfather II*."

"You guys have bodyguards on your *roof?*"

"Focus here, Theo." She rapped me on the skull. "We've got to move that armoire again."

Somehow the armoire had gotten heavier since we left. We inched it aside with even less finesse than before, certain with every scrape that the police would somehow hear us and track the noises to Jack's room.

With not a second to spare, I burst through the connecting door again. But this time, a light beckoned me at the other end of the closet. Where I saw Madame Dumont, sunken to the floor, the cardigan she'd come back for forgotten, my very own painting held in her arms while tears streamed down her face.

Chapter Eighteen

You may have figured out by now that Anna Trenczer was none other than my next-door neighbor, Madame Dumont. I didn't until that very moment. And my grandfather certainly never did.

In retrospect, it seems fitting that the very girl Jack hoped to rescue was hiding at arm's reach: across that fence, behind that blockaded connecting door, inside that prim, prickly exterior that drove him farther away. They emerged from the war just alike, my grandfather and Anna—each captive in a prison of their own distrust, determined never to leave their fate or freedom in anyone's hands but their own.

So was it providence that brought her to the house right next door? Destiny? A mind-blowing co-incidence? Not really, as it turns out.

It seems the house next door wasn't just any

boardinghouse. Jack, after a decade spent searching for Anna Trenczer on various refugee lists, made a deal with a European relief agency. They could use 20 Spinney Lane, rent free, as a resettlement house for postwar refugees—so long as they were all girls between the ages of sixteen and twenty-four (the age Anna Trenczer would be at the time). Seeing as how this request raised a few eyebrows, he agreed never to enter the house or speak to the girls, but to only communicate through the house matron, who was directed to ask each girl if she knew—or was—Anna Trenczer.

The plan worked. Sort of. Because Anna Trenczer *did* walk through the doors of 20 Spinney Lane sometime in the early 1960s, a recently emancipated orphan from war-torn France.

It's just that the now-grown Anne-Marie Dumont had no memory of ever being Anna Trenczer. Until she saw the painting.

"It was in a suitcase," she recalled slowly, her French-inflected whispers transporting us from her chintz-ruffled bedroom to the scene of her suffering. "We were allowed to bring only one suitcase with us, you see, and my father gave me his, though it was almost as big as me. He pulled out the—how do you say?—the lining and sewed the painting inside, and my mother put the clothing all around to protect it. 'A man will come to for you,' my father said. 'He will wear a uniform with lightning on his collar. Give him the suitcase, and he will take you out of here.'

"That was in the camp. A crowded, disgusting place, not fit for human beings. But they didn't treat us as human beings, so perhaps it was appropriate in their eyes. Before that—I can still see it—there had been a grand apartment with a lot of lovely things. Books, silver, art on every wall. And toys, so many toys." Madame Dumont sighed to think of it. "Now we were sleeping twenty to a tiny room, all of us living out of the one suitcase we were allowed. No working toilets, no washroom. We all had lice, and the hallways and stairways, disgusting with human waste . . ."

Madame Dumont shook her head. "Ah, but I would have stopped time and made that our eternity, if I could. Because my mother and father were with me there.

"They took the mothers and fathers away, you see. The children left behind. Can you imagine?" She looked from me, to Bodhi, who had crept in behind me. "Children no older than you, watching over hundreds of little ones.

"The big children said we were going on the

trains next. We waited and waited every day for an announcement. And then one day, they called my name. Mine alone. There was a man in a uniform like my father described. He said he needed to take me to a different camp. He smiled a lot with teeth so straight and white; he seemed so . . . golden next to my rags. The man signed a few papers, then put his hand on my shoulder and took me out through the front gates. At his car, he took the suitcase from my hands and picked me up and hid me in the trunk under a blanket.

"We took a long, bumpy drive, and when the man opened the trunk, it was completely dark. We were behind the gates of an enclosed building—a convent, I learned. I had never been inside one before. The man handed some papers to a nun, who gave him a sort of blessing. Then he turned and went to his car. He did not look at me again.

"From that moment I was Anne Dumont, the name on my false papers. I stayed there, a convent girl now, until I was eighteen."

"But Anne-Marie . . . ?" I broke in.

"My baptismal name. The nuns baptized me, you see, when it was time for the First Communion. Otherwise the girls would know that I was . . . different."

What do you know? Goldie had been on the right track.

Madame Dumont looked right at me with her shining, distant eyes. "I don't remember my name, you know. Or theirs . . . my parents."

I took a tentative step closer and lowered down to my knees, too, as if approaching a strange puppy. "Max," I said quietly. "Max Trenczer. That was your father." I stopped there. The story about Max and Jack's friendship could wait.

"Tren-cher." Madame Dumont echoed my pronunciation, tilting one ear up. "Anne—Anna *Trawnshair*," she repeated, with a French inflection this time, and nodded slowly. "Yes. Yes, I remember it now."

"And you remember the painting?" Bodhi ventured gently from behind me.

Madame Dumont released her hold on the canvas slowly, holding it out at arm's length. "At the camp, I carried the suitcase with me wherever I went. The other children teased me, accused me of hiding food or even gold. Once some boys took it away and tried to open it, break the lock. But it was a strong, expensive suitcase. The lock had three numbers to dial: three-one-zero, my birthday, October third."

She smiled. "It was a hot summer, just like this one. One could not sleep with twenty in a room. So every morning I woke before the sun and went quietly to the window. I would open the suitcase and pull out the thread?—no, the stitches—of the lining again, just to let the dawn light the painting inside."

Madame Dumont lightly traced the surface with her fingertips. "This face became my mother's face. I am ashamed to say that it did not take long before I forgot how she looked. But this one. She looked at me—you see, she still does—with worry and pain and, oh, such an aching love. It was a strange comfort, to think that someone would grieve for me, too."

"Grieve for you?" I asked.

"Of course." Madame Dumont looked at me. "I knew I would be dead quite soon. Like my parents. And like the baby in the painting."

Chapter Nineteen

Madame Dumont was right. Raphael's child, the drawn, wasted child sprawled on his mother's lap, had not been sleeping. He was dead.

It had been right there on the surface (well, under the egg, technically) all along. Once we'd gotten Madame Dumont settled with a cup of tea and her beloved painting, I went home and dug out Reverend Cecily's notes from the bottom of my sweater bag. She was right: the poem said it all.

The baby was indeed the "bread of life" in question, brought into the world by Raphael's favorite "baker": La Fornarina. But, as the poem tells us, his soul ascended to heaven before he could grow up: "risen yet unrisen." And the experience of having a son must have deeply touched Raphael, nourishing

and comforting even the man who seemingly had
it all.

It wasn't just the poem. The painting's message
was in every corner of the painting: the storm clouds
in the distance, the ashen Christ Child. Even Bodhi
had sensed something was wrong with our initial
reading. Yes, that was a dove, but it wasn't descend-
ing from heaven. It was *ascending*, flying away and
leaving this world behind.

Of course, you really didn't need clues or symbol-
ism at all. The entire painting lay in La Fornarina's
face, stricken with grief. How did I miss it? Maybe it's
that the faces of mothers I see are more consumed
with worry about their kid's pineapple allergy or pre-
school applications. Or in the case of my mother,
the mechanics of number theory and her dwindling
tea stash.

But a sixteenth-century audience knew what a
grieving mother looked like. And so did Anna.

I think grief transformed Raphael, too. He may
have initially tried to hide his family from society,
but ultimately he refused to let his child go to the
grave in secret. In those final days of the child's ill-
ness, Raphael immortalized the boy and his family
through one real, unidealized painting: a painting

that showed things as they really were and not how his patrons wished things to be.

Or at least, he tried to. Because when Raphael himself died not long afterward, the assistants from his studio sprang into action. After first packing Margherita Luti off to a local convent, they set to work painting out all evidence of La Fornarina's marriage to Raphael, thereby preserving their teacher's, and their own, reputation.

(That family portrait must have proven particularly challenging, requiring his workshop to cover up an entire self-portrait of their master with a single, withered tree.)

It worked. Because Raphael died young, he left behind a limited pool of unsold works. His reputation sterling and his works now rare, all of Europe went wild to secure a Raphael. The value of his paintings only rose from that point forward. The artists of Raphael's workshop went on to successful careers of their own. And a young widow lived out the rest of her days in a Roman nunnery, just another girl whose secret was guarded by the convent walls.

In the end, the painting was priceless.

Quite literally. Because, despite all the tests and

authentications and expert opinions and, don't forget, groundbreaking discoveries of two thirteen-year-old girls, no one ever placed a single bid.

The painting never saw the light of an auction block. Once Madame Dumont got back that last link to her missing childhood, she wasn't about to let it go. She even dug into her newly released store of generosity to host a viewing party at her tea shop one crisp Sunday afternoon that fall. She let Bodhi and me make the guest list, inviting all the people who aided in solving its mystery. Mr. Katsanakis offered to cater.

"It's all my fault, you know," said Bodhi, nursing a cup of Indian chai in one hand and brushing spanakopita crumbs off her shirt with the other.

"What's your fault?" I said. "Stick to the stuffed grape leaves, by the way."

"Remember when I made that wish at the Temple of Dendur at the Met?" She snagged a dolmade as a plate sailed by. "I wished for the painting to be priceless. And now I guess it is, because we'll never know what it would've gone for."

After the discovery in Madame Dumont's closet, we'd been able to appeal to Goldie for guidance. Goldie hooked Madame Dumont up with a pro-bono lawyer who specialized in Holocaust restitution rights. That lawyer suggested we get the painting to an auction house ASAP for testing and appraisal and recommended a guy she knew: Augustus Garvey at Cadwalader's. Reverend Cecily's friend and Gemma's boss. Gus ended up being a really nice guy who'd studied his way out of the wrong side of the Bronx. We hit it off right away.

"It's not you, Bodhi," Gus explained, blowing on a peppermint tisane. "I don't know that it would've sold anyway. There comes a point when there is just not enough groundswell of confidence to tip the scales. Who wants to be the only institution to gamble millions of dollars, not knowing if anyone else is willing to pay it? No," he mused, "I don't think there's enough scientific evidence in the world to authenticate a discovery this big."

The painting loomed over us from a spot on the wall over the cash register, still as melancholy as ever. But the crowd was here to celebrate.

Reverend Cecily sat drawing out stories from Mo, who had been brought by his daughter, and *her* son, and *his* twins, who were in turn distracted from their great-grandfather's tales by their strategic position next to the cake table.

Bodhi's parents were there, too, her dad signing autographs, her mom in a corner captivated by my mom, whom we'd coaxed into a dress and out of the house. I wanted to think that they were trading stories about their ingenious daughters, but I'm pretty sure Jessica Blake was just studying her for an upcoming part as an eccentric recluse.

Sanjiv alternated between cornering Cadwalader lab technicians and refilling bowls with Toasty Nuts.

Goldie and Eddie had found a table away from the action, where they murmured sweet talk about archival storage and database management.

Even Lydon was there, aggressively courting Madame Dumont in hopes of a future donation of the unsold Raphael. ("Are you nuts?" I said when Bodhi suggested inviting him. "Hey, if he hadn't shown up at your house, you never would've moved the painting into Dumont's closet and the mystery never would've been solved." She had a point. "Also," she continued, "we can rub his face in it.")

Whenever I attempted to get more hummus or find the bathroom, I was stopped by someone with a word or pat on the back or a "Can you believe . . . ?" I'd already received an invitation to both Bodhi's and Mr. K's for dinner, a nonnegotiable mandate to raid the Grace Church food pantry, and, most incredibly, an afterschool job offer.

Well, because of child labor laws, an unpaid internship, really. But an internship that carried a transportation stipend: twenty dollars that would stay right in my pocket each day as I made the long walk home from Cadwalader's. Yes, Cadwalader's. Gus had asked me to assist him three afternoons a week. You can guess how long it took me to accept.

It seemed so long ago that I could walk the streets of New York an entire day without uttering a word to anyone. So long ago that Jack and I had barricaded ourselves in our little fortress of self-reliance, scavenging the city for crumbs. But since Jack's death, the city had changed. I had changed. Now, when I ventured out, I saw not crumbs, but a feast of possibilities.

Bodhi was right. The mystery was always bigger than just me. Somehow, along the way, I had become part of the city. And it had become part of me.

Thanksgiving

By November, I had a lot to be thankful for.

We'd had a fairly meager harvest after that hot summer, but I'd finally taken up Reverend Cecily's offer of the church food pantry, which allowed us to experience the wonders of boxed mac and cheese and lots of tuna fish alongside our pickled beets.

Another score: Madame Dumont had waived all of my mother's past and future tea purchases. So Mom was kept happy through the chilly fall with infinite pots of hot tea.

I still had Bodhi. We'd gotten used to the paparazzi buzzing around, although they soon discovered that Bodhi didn't vary her new uniform (now from her private school) anymore than the old one. (For my part, I'd started reworking the attic's castoffs into a fall wardrobe, including something I call "faux-veralls.")

I had my internship at Cadwalader's, where a different art history mystery awaited me every time I walked in Gus's office. I loved it.

But there was only so far my weekly taxi stipend could take me. Which is why, as of Thanksgiving, the heat was still shut off and our holiday feast consisted of rice, beans, and packaged stuffing from the food pantry.

After our early and brief dinner, Mom retreated to her room and I headed to Jack's studio. The summer's breezes were long gone, replaced by chilling gusts that rattled the windowpanes. But in the late afternoon, the sun's last rays came bursting through the windows, creating a greenhouse effect of light and warmth.

Like a cat, I stretched out on my belly and surfed the sunbeams as they crept across the floor, my book open in front of me. It was one that Gus had recommended to prep for some Flemish still lifes that were coming in from the London office, and I was soaking in the ornate details when the sunbeams dried up, instantly transforming the light-drenched studio into a cold and drafty garret.

Shivering, I looked up at the fireplace and wondered if there was any reason I couldn't build a fire. To be fair, I'd never seen Jack do it, and I imagined the chimney had been bricked in. Or maybe he'd been reluctant to make the paint-strewn room any more flammable than it already was. Wrapping myself in a quilt I'd dragged up, I crept over to investigate more closely and was surprised to see a visible crack, maybe an eighth of an inch wide, between the marble mantel top and the mantelpiece below.

On closer inspection, it appeared that the mantel top had been raised a couple of inches with a piece of wood. In all my searches this summer, I'd never noticed it. It had been polished and painted to such an impeccable faux finish that it exactly matched the marble that sandwiched it. I ran my fingertip along the crack, then wedged my fingernail underneath the mantel top. It shifted ever so slightly.

As the wind howled at the windows, I realized suddenly that it had loosened the mantel as well. The heat and humidity must have swollen the wood all summer, wedging the marble in. But now, with the cold, dry air filling the studio, the wood was contracting, revealing a seam that begged to be opened.

I carefully picked up my grandmother's bowl and Adelaide's egg and set them down next to my book.

The mantel, while heavy, lifted up fairly easily once I figured out where to grab hold. I set that on the floor, too, then peered inside the marble mantelpiece.

Right there, under the egg. Just as Jack had promised.

It was a space about four inches deep, filled neatly with stacks of one-hundred-dollar bills, laid side by side like sardines in a can. I started to count the rubber-banded bundles—one thousand, ten thousand, twenty, thirty, one hundred thousand!—when I came to a yellowed envelope.

The front was addressed in flowing, fountain pen script to "Angelika." That name had been crossed out with ballpoint, and written over with "Theo."

It was a letter from Jack, of course.

My dearest one,

If you have found this letter, it means that I am dead.

It also means that you have found the money. This—and the house—is all I have to leave you, and I have worked hard to maintain it, occasionally to add to it, a little here and there whenever I could. If you treat it the same way, working hard to save it and add to it, it will live on indefinitely.

I make only one stipulation. As I write this, I have spent thirty years—here the *"thirty"* had been crossed out with ballpoint again and replaced with *"sixty"*—attempting to right a wrong. I am asking you to succeed where I have failed.

First, some background:

Like many men, I went to Europe in the war. There I had the misfortune of being taken prisoner and interned in a Nazi work camp called Berga. I was one of the lucky ones. I was assigned to kitchen duty, while friends and fellow soldiers fell almost daily to the inhuman conditions in the mines where they worked. This was the greatest lesson of war, in my estimation: the entirely arbitrary line between life and death.

At Berga, I met a man named Max Trenczer. He was a Jew from Paris who owned a successful gallery under his own name. Please make a note of this.

Max was an extraordinary man—brilliant, witty, brave—and I wish you could have met him. We made a plan to run away from this camp, but he was caught as we tried to escape, and instead

*of stopping to fight or even help, I am ashamed to
say that I fled to save my own life.*

*But that is my own burden. While in the camp,
Max told me how, before the Nazis invaded and
took over his business, an aristocratic Italian
gentleman brought in a few paintings to sell.
He was hoping to stockpile some cash before the
impending war. Max was intrigued by one work
in particular, not just because of its distinctive
style, but also because of its cryptic inscription. He
had reason to believe the painting was a missing
work by Raphael, and because the Italian did not
know anything of the painting's origins, Max was
able to buy it for a very good price.*

*Max had planned to confirm its authenticity
and sell it on the open market. But then the war
broke out. He was able to hide the painting as
the Nazis seized his gallery, and because of his
friendship with a Nazi officer—everyone, even
Nazis, loved Max—he was able to trade the
painting for his daughter's escape.*

*His daughter's name was Anna. Anna
Trenczer. Please make a note of this name also.*

*Now imagine my shock when, after finding
my way back to the Allies and a newly formed
division of art experts, I was cataloging Hitler's*

personal art collection and stumbled upon a work matching, down to the very last detail, Max's own painting.

I thought at first of appealing to my commanding officer (a man you now know as "Uncle" Lydon). Unlike the many other ownerless works of art, which flooded us in wave after wave of shipments, I actually knew this painting's owner.

But before I could speak up, I noticed something curious. Lydon, and many of his cronies, did not seem very interested in finding the owners of these works. They made some nominal effort at restitution, but ultimately, an orphaned work could be absorbed into a museum's collection for "safekeeping." And just how much effort do you think these museums would go to, finding the long-lost relatives of a long-dead owner, when they could instead keep selling tickets to see their newfound Rembrandt, Vermeer, Leonardo . . . or Raphael?

I saw other items pouring in, too—not just paintings and sculpture, but rugs, silverware, antiques, jewelry, even silver menorahs, bells stripped from Torahs. Personal—very personal— items, but with real, concrete value. Belongings that could have been traded for a man, woman, or child's freedom.

I saw that returning Max's painting wasn't a simple matter of property rights. It was a matter of self-determination. With that painting in his possession, Max had had the power to determine one young girl's destiny.

And now I could restore that power.

I said nothing to Lydon. I quietly removed the painting from the collection, changed its records to read "damaged beyond repair," and began to plot how to bring it back home with me.

I worried that my bags or shipments home would be checked and the painting found. Luckily, I had worked at a paint store in New York where the owner had been working on a new water-based polymer paint formulation whose key feature was—unlike oil—its easy removal. I asked him to send over samples and then used them to paint my own composition over the canvas below. From there, I was able to camouflage it quite easily among several other original paintings and smuggle it past any curious military police.

That's where my luck ended. Despite my efforts with various refugee organizations over the years, I have not found Anna Trenczer. The fact that her painting ended up in Hitler's own collection means that the trade was made. I am guessing

*her escape may not have gone through traditional
channels; it's likely she was smuggled out of the
country, possibly without papers or passport.*

*But back to the purpose for this letter. My
search has ended. Yours is just beginning.*

*Find a bottle of basic rubbing alcohol and some
rags. Take down the painting that hangs over
the fireplace in my studio, the one with the egg.
(This part may be difficult for you, but trust me.)
If you soak a rag in the alcohol and slowly blot
the surface of the painting, my own composition
should lift off easily, revealing the original
painting underneath. Enjoy. I have not seen it
since those days in Germany, but I remember it
was quite stunning.*

*Now you will know what you are working for.
Your mission differs somewhat from mine. I was
looking for the painting's owner. You will look for
the painting's home. Anna Trenczer may or may
not be alive, but I have to believe that some relative,
no matter how distant, survived somewhere on that
vast continent. Find that person. Give them back the
power to determine their own path.*

*One final note: I do not care about my own
reputation. Perhaps, in your efforts, you may have
to reveal my misdeeds, and hear me slandered as a*

thief or a speculator. But I can tell you truly that,
when you have survived a man-wrought machine
that enslaved others for its bidding, murdered
them for its pleasure, and sentenced the survivors
to a lifetime of haunted memories, you have no
appetite left for anything but freedom. And that I
have enjoyed in endless amounts.

Your loving Jack

The ballpoint pen appeared again here, in a post-
script written in a shakier hand:

My only Theodora,

I wrote this letter for your mother when she was
young. Now I know that you are the one I was
waiting for.
I told you once that your mother was a
songbird, but you are a chicken. Just like me. We
dig in, we roost, we never stop scratching until we
find what we're looking for.

Dig, Theodora. Look under the egg and dig deep.

Acknowledgments

O ne of my favorite writers, Umberto Eco, wrote that "Books always speak of other books." In this case, *Under the Egg* was born on page thirty-five of another great art history mystery: *The Forger's Spell* by Edward Dolnick.

The Forger's Spell tells the true story of the man who forged and sold Vermeers to the Nazis (referenced by Theo as she conducts her own research). I was riveted by the stranger-than-fiction story when I stopped at this section:

The easiest test of an old master—and the one test almost certain to be carried out—is to dab the surface with rubbing alcohol. In a genuinely old painting, the surface will be hard, and the alcohol will have no effect. If the painting is new, the alcohol will dissolve a bit of paint, and the tester's cotton swab will come up smudged with color.

Those three sentences sparked an idea—what if someone deliberately painted over an old master, knowing that they could remove the top layer and leave the original untouched?—and set my mind off and running down the path of forgeries, smuggling, and ultimately Nazi art theft.

Over the course of the following months, three other sources became invaluable. First, a fascinating documentary called *The Rape of Europa*, based on the exhaustively, exactingly researched book by Lynn H. Nicholas. That led me to Robert M. Edsel's *The Monuments Men*, and then *Soldiers and Slaves* by Roger Cohen, one of the first sources to unveil the abuses at the forgotten Berga labor camp. I highly recommend these excellent books to anyone who wants to know the real-life stories behind Jack's adventure.

Like Theo, my progress depended on New York City's great research institutions: namely, the Metropolitan Museum of Art and the Center for Jewish History. But one institution stands in a class all its own. Thank you to the Brooklyn Public Library, where my fortune in library fines couldn't begin to repay my gratitude for their online hold system and generous checkout policies. (Did you know you can take out ninety-nine items at a time?!?)

Also like Theo, I am grateful to live in this vibrant city where every interaction sparks ideas and writing leads. Special thanks go to the many people who offered information and insight along the way: Paul Griffin, Marianna Baer, Nancy Mercado, Barbara Veith, Ian Ehling, Carrie Peterson, Morris Marx, Geoffrey Marx, Susan Hawk, Jason and Shira Koch Epstein, not to mention my Latin consultants, Andrew Durbin and Nina Quirk-Goldblatt.

I am beyond blessed to have found two partners who believed in my egg-in-the-rough even more than I did. Thank you, Sara Crowe, for sending me the best e-mail I've ever gotten, and thank you, Nancy Conescu, for the gentle and gracious way you pushed to make each draft better.

Finally, thank you to my smart, creative, and endlessly patient husband, Dave, who cheerfuly slogged through many drafts, contributing a critical eye and nifty plot points along the way. Never has a cliché been so true: I couldn't have done it without you.